Walking After Midnight: Tales of the Paranormal

by Evan Camby

For K & S, constant encouragers of creativity.

Thanks for letting me be weird.

Table of Contents

"One need not be a chamber to be haunted,

One need not be a house;

The brain has corridors surpassing

Material place."

Emily Dickinson

CABIN CREEK

At some point, evil beckons for all of us. It calls us by name, and it shows up dressed as our favorite sins. When it does, we have the choice to answer the call or to fight. When evil came for Sheriff Earl Benoit one cool September evening, he answered, and he's answered ever since.

It began with the animals. Old lady Harlan's little toy poodle went missing from her backyard. Not so strange, in a rural town. Coyotes, foxes, even a large hawk could snatch up an ankle-biter like Snickers. But when the cows turned up missing, or worse, were found with huge chunks of flesh taken out of them, that's when Earl had to do something.

Doug Beck walked into the Sheriff's office without knocking, wringing his cap in his hands. He sat down and looked at the floor for a few minutes without speaking.

"What is it?" Earl asked, trying to mask the concern in his voice. Autumn wind flowed through the office window, banging the blinds against the frame.

Doug finally looked up from the floor. "That was my last cow, Earl. What am I supposed to do? We can't afford another, not now."

Benoit swiveled in his chair and looked out the window. The trees had turned a flaming shade of crimson, signaling the beginning of the cold season. He watched a few leaves fall to the ground and drummed his fingers on the table. "Suppose'n it's vandals. What then?"

"Vandals? Christ! You know what this is about, Earl. Just as plain as day, you know." The farmer stood up from the chair and headed out of the office. Before leaving, he turned around and said, "You best deal with this. I got a mind to start letting folks in on our little secret, otherwise."

The Sheriff watched his cousin walk out of the office and swiveled back around to face the door, his jaw clenched. He knew what was happening, and he knew how to stop it. But he never would—and no matter the cost, Earl Benoit would take this secret to his grave.

* * *

In the summer of 1959, Doug and Earl were celebrating their ninth birthdays at a joint celebration thrown by their mothers—twin sisters with long hair as black as pitch.

"Make a wish, boys!" Earl's mom, Crystal, said as she set a chocolate sheet cake on the picnic table in the front yard. A few of their friends were gathered around wearing plastic cowboy hats and clutching cap guns.

A man in a white Chrysler sedan came careening around the corner, weaved down the road, and came to a stop with its front wheels on the grass of the front yard. He stumbled out of the car dressed in a cheap brown suit, glass bottles tumbling out with him, and made his way towards Doug's mother, Nadine.

She spotted him, and her eyes bulged. Standing up, she immediately turned to run into the house, but the man caught her by the lapels of her dress and pulled her face close to his.

Without a word, he swung one arm around and punched her in the jaw. Nadine crumbled to the ground in a heap, and Crystal ran over and jumped on the man's back.

"Harvey, stop it! Get off of her!" she screamed, placing both her hands around his neck and squeezing. With little effort, the man threw her off and stumbled into the house. She got to her feet and scurried to Nadine, who was laying unconscious on the ground.

Doug and Earl began to cry, and so did most of their friends. It was the last time either of them celebrated a birthday.

* * *

That night, Earl woke up to whispering coming from somewhere in the house. He tip-toed out of bed and peered into the hallway. It was dark, but a sliver of light spilled out of the door that led down to the basement. He took one look back at Doug, still asleep in the bed next to his, and then stepped carefully out of their room. On his way to the basement door, he peeked his head into Nadine's room and saw Harvey passed out on the bed, still wearing his brown suit. A bottle of bourbon laid next to him, some of it spilling out and forming a pool on the hardwood. The entire room reeked of cheap liquor. Harvey snored and rolled over onto his stomach.

Earl sneered at him before beginning his walk down the hallway towards the basement door. The whispering sound was growing louder, more melodic. He reached one hand for the doorknob and pulled it open. It creaked slightly, and he winced. Earl stood as still as stone for a minute, but the whispering continued. He took a careful step down the basement stairway.

As he crossed the threshold, ice-cold air spilled over him, and the whispering whirled around his body like gusts of wind. Earl strained his ears, trying to make sense of the words, but they didn't sound like anything he had ever heard. He continued down the stairs and finally made it to the bottom, where he carefully peeked around the corner.

The young boy had to bring a hand to his mouth to keep from gasping.

Crystal and Nadine sat across from one another wearing white shift gowns. They were holding hands, and between them sat a large boiling pot, the one they usually kept over the stove. Black steam rose out of it and formed sinister shapes in the air, which pulsed and grew with their chanting. They formed a black cloud and rose, hovering above the sisters as they spoke. Strands of their black hair floated around them like slithering snakes, as if a strong wind were flowing through the basement.

Their chanting grew louder, and with it, the black cloud above them grew. Crystal and Nadine were now practically shouting the words in a rough, stilted language and, as much as Earl strained his ears, he couldn't understand a word of it. He gasped and took a step back, knocking a little clay pot over with his foot. It crashed on the dirt floor of the basement and both sisters jerked their heads to follow the noise.

Earl shrieked. Their eyes were milky white, with no trace of their bright-blue irises. He turned and raced up the stairs, bounded down the hall to his room, and dove under the covers. Until the light shone through his bedroom window at dawn, he lay there, frozen.

* * *

It was hunger that finally prodded Earl out of his room. He tiptoed down the hallway towards the kitchen, relieved that he could hear the normal, cheerful sounds of breakfast. Plates clinked against the table, bacon sizzled and popped on a cast-iron skillet, and the pages of a newspaper crinkled loudly as Crystal shuffled through them.

For a moment, Earl allowed himself to believe it had all been a dream, and he stepped cautiously into the kitchen. That hope was dashed when both women stopped what they were doing and jerked their heads towards him with stern, knowing eyes.

"Good morning, Earl," his mother said primly through a thin-lipped smile.

He shuffled to the table and kept his eyes on the ground.

"Good morning, Momma. Good morning, Aunt Nadine."

His mom put a plate in front of him, two eggs with toast and bacon. It was the same breakfast he had every day, but something was very wrong. His mother was staring, so he picked up a fork and took a bite, forcing a smile. "Where's Doug?" he asked.

Nadine turned from the kitchen window to face her nephew. She was playing with the collar of her robe as she drilled her eyes into his. "We sent Doug to the market for a few things. Your mother and I thought we could talk to you for a spell before he gets back."

Doug paused his fork in mid-air and looked at the two women. He had thought he was going to be in trouble, but it was suddenly clear that they were more frightened than he was. "Alright," he said, setting the fork down.

His mother grabbed his hand and sat down next to him at the table, eyeing him with hopeful concern, as if she was about to trust him with a secret. Nadine sat down on the other side of Earl and looked at them both.

"Honey," his mother started, "We saw you last night. In the basement. You were watching us, yes?"

Doug's eyes went huge. He had been clinging to the hope that what he saw had been some kind of nightmare. His mouth parted slightly as he nodded at the women.

"Shouldn't have been sneaking around," Nadine chimed in.

Crystal shot her a look and took her son's chin in her hand and guided his face so that he was staring her right in the eyes. "What you saw—what you *think* you saw down there. You can tell no one about that, not even your cousin. You understand?"

"I won't, Momma," he said. "But what were—"

Nadine reached across the table and grabbed his arm, digging her nails into the skin a bit. Doug looked at his aunt, at her yellowish-purple left eye, now swollen from where Harvey had punched her. Normally, she hid for a day or so when Harvey did things like that, but today, she somehow looked proud. "That doesn't concern you," she said. "Everything is going to be alright now."

The women shared a look that Earl couldn't quite read, and it chilled him. These women who had raised him looked different somehow, foreign and ghoulish in their joint solemnity and insistence that he kept what he had seen to himself. For the first time, he was afraid of them.

Earl swallowed hard. "I won't say nothin, I swear."

For a split second, Crystal's lip trembled as she looked at her son, and she stood to press his head against her stomach before he could see her cry. Nadine got up from the table and walked back to her bedroom. Then it was just the boy and his mother in the small kitchen. She brushed a hand through his hair.

"Thank you, honey," Crystal whispered. "Thank you."

* * *

No one ever saw Harvey alive again. The police came to the house after his boss reported him missing, but it only happened once and he only asked a few questions. Doug watched from behind the couch as the tall officer with shiny buttons talked to his mom and aunt in the front of the house.

"Ladies, thank you for your time," he said, tipping his hat before he left.

Doug could have sworn the man winked at his aunt Nadine on his way out the door.

After the officer left, Earl only heard the women mention Harvey once more. It was the following day, and he was playing on the floor of his room as his mom and aunt folded laundry down the hall.

"That's the problem with being a professional sonofabitch— you go missing and no one misses you at all."

The women shared a short laugh as Doug stood up, suddenly uneasy, shutting his bedroom door.

Three days later, some locals found Harvey's body. It was bloated and floating in a wide part of Cabin Creek, snagged on a small tree which had fallen into the water.

Only Nadine, Crystal, Doug, and Earl attended the small funeral. Afterwards, they followed the hearse to the old Cabin Creek Cemetery out past State Road 39. The preacher tossed dirt on the coffin as they lowered it into the ground, and when he said, "Ashes to ashes, dust to dust," Doug caught his mother and Nadine sharing a tiny, knowing smile.

For a while afterwards, life was normal. Doug and Earl started school that fall, and things were quiet for almost a year. When the one-year anniversary of Harvey's death rolled around, that's when it happened.

Evil came calling.

* * *

"Earl, wake up!"

Earl squinted through half-awake eyes at his cousin's tear-streaked face. "It's my mom—help—wake up!"

He shot out of bed and followed Doug down the hallway, watching in horror as his cousin flung the basement door open and shot downstairs. A vision of what he had seen a year ago, right before Harvey's death, flashed in his eyes, and his stomach flipped. The boys ran down the stairs, and as they did, Doug's cries mixed with Crystal's.

When they got to her, she was hugging Nadine's lifeless body on the dirt floor. A large bite had been taken out of her neck, as if an animal had mauled her. Doug vomited, and Earl rushed over to his mom. She was weeping silently, brushing the hair from her sister's face and rocking her.

"What happened?" Earl cried, but his mother ignored him. "Momma!" he begged.

Crystal let her sister's body slip from her arms and looked up at her son in grim resolution. "We messed up, son. Your aunt and I broke the rules, and she paid for it. God forgive me, she paid for it," she said. "Doug, go upstairs and call for an ambulance. Earl, stay down here with me for a minute. Be a good boy, now." Her eyes were blank and her voice was toneless. Earl looked at his mother, now nearly dead behind the eyes, and wished that she had sent him up to call for the ambulance instead of his cousin.

He heard Doug march up the basement stairs and watched his mother for a few seconds before reluctantly walking towards her. Blood from Nadine's wound stained the front of her floral day dress. The red stood out in contrast to the light blue fabric with green flowers printed on it. Doug tried to focus on the flowers, to grasp at something pleasant and familiar, but the blood jumped out at him.

"Come closer, baby," his mom said, her voice hollow. He stepped closer, avoiding looking at the huge chunk of flesh missing from his aunt's neck.

"Honey," she continued, "You remember that night, don't you? Yes, I know you do." She raised one hand to the side of her mouth and furrowed her brow. "I was sorry you had to see it, but now… now you can understand… now it's good that you saw."

Doug knew he was watching his mother unravel, and he was more frightened than he had ever been. She gripped his arm tightly and spoke in a rushed, whispered tone.

"Your grandmother taught your Aunt Nadine and I how to… take care of certain things. Certain people. Her mother taught her, as did her mother before that. Nadine's friend, Harvey? He was a wicked man. And he needed to be taken care of."

Sirens sounded off from far away, and Crystal quickened the pace of her story.

"But listen to me, we did something wrong—missed some step, I'm not sure. He came back, Earl! Do you understand? Do you know what you have to do?"

Earl shook his head in fear and confusion and said, "Momma, I don't know what you mean." He cried.

"Make him rest, son," she said.

A knock came from the door upstairs and Earl heard boots pounding on the living room floor.

His mother grabbed him by the shirt. "It's all in the book," she said, pointing underneath the basement staircase. "Find the book, and make him rest!" she cried.

The officers came down the stairs, and Earl heard them speak for the first time. "Miss Crystal, please let the boy go."

Her eyes stayed locked on her son, pleading silently. *Make him rest.*

"Let him go, Crystal!"

A gun cocked.

A pair of hands grabbed Earl by the shirt, pulling him away from his mother, and led him up the stairs.

It was the last time he ever saw her alive.

* * *

Sheriff Earl Benoit looked out the window of his office as he remembered that day, still trying to forget the way the blood soaked into his mother's floral dress. The day after they took his mom away, they had sent him and Earl to live with a distant cousin, a farmer, on the outskirts of Cabin Creek. A week after that, the school principal had called him down to his office. The memory was still vibrant after all these years. Earl could still hear the sound his sneakers made as he walked the long hallway to Mr. Lowry's office.

He didn't even have to open the door. The secretary was waiting and pulled it open before Earl's hand reached for the knob. The dowdy woman motioned for him to walk in with an unusually kind look on her face. Earl and his friends called the old spinster "Lowry's Witch" because of her appearance, but today she looked softer somehow. Earl nodded at the woman and continued past her desk into the principal's office.

The man sat, tall and gangly, in an executive chair with his hands pressed together in front of his face like a church steeple. He lowered them and spoke to the freckle-faced boy in front of his desk. "Close the door, son," he said.

Earl did as he was told, sitting down in a creaky student's chair in front of the desk. The man studied him, and the boy stared right back. Sternness had set wrinkles deep into the principal's face, but today, at least, Earl was relieved that he did not look angry.

"Son, I'm afraid I have some bad news. It's about your mother. Now, you know she was very sick—"

The boy gulped as the floor seemed to drop from underneath him. Suddenly the only thing he could think of was the wild look in his mother's eyes in the basement that day, the way she had gripped his arm, pleading with him.

"Make him rest."

"—time to be a man now. You understand?"

Earl nodded blankly, but suddenly it felt like he was in a tunnel which blurred out the sounds of Lowry speaking. Something was wrong with Momma. He tried to make sense of the words he was hearing, but they somehow seemed nonsensical. The spaces around his periphery darkened, and he gripped the sides of the chair.

"Mr. Lowry, I'm not feeling very…"

* * *

Earl was back in his mother's basement. It was foggy, and he waved his hands in front of his face to clear the air.

"Momma?"

He heard a sound behind him, like feet shuffling along the dirt floor, and turned around.

Harvey stood there, skin waxy and ashen, peeling off of his skull in patches, wearing the same brown suit they had buried him last year. Earl felt himself freeze as he looked at the man. His face was set with deep wrinkles caked in dirt, and his lips were a grotesque gray.

"Make him rest, Earl!"

Earl whipped around to see his mother coming from the foggy corner of the basement, her hands outstretched, pointing at something beneath the basement stairs.

"Momma, I don't understand—"

Suddenly, she rushed towards him, her palms outstretched. Deep vertical slashes caked in dried blood lined her forearms. Earl screamed and tried to back away, but she grabbed him by the shirt. Her face was close to his as she screamed.

"Make him rest!"

* * *

Earl woke up in the hospital to the beeping of a monitor next to his bed. He was alone in the dimly lit room except for his cousin, who sat next to him looking grave and worried, a strange amount of severity to his face for a boy of eleven.

They stared at each other for a moment before Doug spoke up. "Crystal—"

"She's dead. Ain't she?" Earl asked, his voice shaking.

Doug nodded.

"Listen, I gotta do something," Earl said, "And I think it's real important. To both our moms. But I'm going to need your help."

Doug nodded, furrowing his brow. "Who did this, did your mom say? Is that what she told you when my mom died? Is that why she sent me upstairs for the ambulance?"

Earl's nostrils flared as he struggled not to cry. He nodded at his cousin, and then a choked sob escaped his lips.

Doug reached out and touched Earl's arm. "I'll help—we'll do it together. Whatever it takes."

* * *

The boys snuck out early that night, thankful that the cousin they were staying with was a heavy sleeper. Together, they walked the three miles back to the house where they used to live with their mothers. Looking around, Doug stepped over the police tape still marking the property and motioned for Earl to follow. The boys crept around the back of the house and punched a hole through the screen door to get into the kitchen. For a moment, both of them just stared at their childhood home.

The sink was still full of dishes, and mold had grown on a loaf of bread Nadine left sitting on the counter. A bunch of bananas had turned black, and fruit flies buzzed in the stale air. The whole place reeked of slow decay.

Earl snapped out of it first. "Come on, we gotta get to the basement," he said, walking down the hallway towards the basement door. Before Earl turned the basement doorknob, a flash of that night came to his mind: his mom and Crystal sitting cross-legged on the floor, the black smoke rising from the pot, the way their hair looked like snakes as it swung wildly in the air.

"Make him rest!"

Earl turned the knob and stepped down the basement stairs, with his cousin close behind. They reached the dirt floor and Earl reached a hand across the wall to flip on the light switch. A dark spot mottled the floor. Crystal's blood. Doug looked away.

"Come on," Earl said, motioning underneath the basement stairs. He pressed both hands against the laminate boards covering the sides of the staircase and felt the material give a bit.

Doug stood watching and then, without a word, swung one arm and plunged it through the boards.

Earl looked at his cousin's face in disbelief and worry, then down at his hand. It was bloody, but Doug simply stood there, panting, close to tears. Earl reached a hand out and touched his cousin's shoulder. Doug looked at him and nodded.

The boys bent down and pried the rest of the boards off of the wall. When the laminate panels were all removed and piled behind them, Earl flashed a light under the dark staircase. A blast of cool wind rushed by, and they shared a look before looking at the spot where Earl was pointing the flashlight.

A small, ancient-looking book sat on the floor. Earl reached one hand to lift it up, and Doug cried out, "Don't!"

"Why the hell not? This is what we came here for, ain't it?" Earl said.

Doug shook his head worriedly at the book. "I don't know. I got a real bad feeling just now when we knocked this wall down."

Earl shook his cousin's hand off the book. "Yeah? Well, I've had a 'bad feeling' since both our moms croaked and we got sent to live with some cousin we don't know from Adam. I get a bad feeling when the kids at school call us orphans. I'm tired of feelin' bad."

Doug looked at his cousin and nodded reluctantly.

With the book in Earl's hands, the boys made their way up the stairs and out of the house. Almost out the door, Doug turned back briefly and craned his neck to look around. He turned back to follow his cousin out of the yard and back to their cousin's farmhouse.

He could not shake the feeling that he had heard footsteps coming down the bedroom hallway.

* * *

The next night, they snuck out again. This time, Earl took the book and a flashlight with them, and they headed to the barn out behind the house. They stood for a few moments in the dewy grass in front of the old wooden barn as Earl waved the flashlight around to find the door in the dark. It creaked as they pried it open. The smell of wet hay and rust and stale air floated out, and Doug coughed, waving a hand in front of his face. Earl walked inside and his cousin followed. The boys climbed an ancient-looking ladder up to the hayloft, and Earl sat down with the book in his lap. Doug knelt down next to him.

Earl ran a hand over the cover and reached a shaky hand to open it to the first page. As he did, the barn door slammed shut, its hinges creaking loudly. Both of them jumped, and Earl gave Doug a reassuring look. He had always been the leader of the two. Doug nodded at him as if to say it was alright to proceed, and both boys lowered their eyes to the book now resting on the wooden planks of the hayloft.

Earl held one side of the book down to keep it flat as the wind flowed through the barn door and stir the surrounding air. It had a dark brown jacket which looked like old, worn leather. A symbol was carved into the leather hide—a cage with a large eyeball inside. Earl put the flashlight in his mouth to free his hands and opened the book.

The pages looked older than any they had ever seen in schoolbooks. They were ivory and jagged on the edges and thick—almost thicker than dollar bills. The pages made a slight crunching sound as they turned, rustling like old leaves. As wind continued to blow through the barn, the pages flipped like a fan. The boys put their hands down to steady it and keep the book from flying off the loft, and both of them saw it at once.

The book had opened to a page with a picture of a man laying lifeless on the ground. The words above the drawing were written an old script which was barely legible.

"Carmine Mortem Ut Inmortui"

The boys looked at it for a second, squinting to see in the dark, then Earl pointed the flashlight closer towards the picture. There were more words under the title.

"Faciam Enim Eum Requiescere"

Underneath those words were several lines of script, all in the same unfamiliar tongue.

"I don't understand," Earl muttered.

"What's wrong?" Doug asked.

Earl shook his head and flipped through the book. "I'm supposed to find something here, but I don't know… I can't read any of it!" his flipping became frantic, and then he slammed the book closed. "Shit!"

Doug flinched. "What were you supposed to find?"

Earl turned to look at his cousin. "When I was in the hospital, Momma came to me. It was like I was back in the house, in the basement, only in a dream. I saw her there, and she spoke to me and then Harvey was in the basement, too. She told me I had to make him rest, and she pointed under the stairs. That's how I knew to look for this, that it would have what we needed—"

"Make who rest?"

Earl looked at him. Doug's eyes went wide.

"No, Earl—he's dead! Harvey is dead!" he said.

"You saw what happened to your mom. That bite on her neck? He came back, Doug! What else could she have meant by 'Make him rest'?"

Just then, another gust of wind flew through the barn and blew the book open to the same page as before, with the man laying on the ground and the words *"Carmine Mortem Ut Inmortui"* printed above him.

"Make him rest!" sounded in Earl's ears. He shone the light on the words to pronounce them. "Carmine Mortem Ut Inmor... Inmor... tooey?"

"Carmen Mortimer Ud Inmortuey?" Doug asked, his face curled up in confusion.

"No, Carmine Mortem Ut Inmortui..." Earl said, trailing off as he looked at the rest of the words. There were five lines of text after it. "It looks like a set of instructions. You know, like when you put a tinker toy together." He turned to look at Doug.

"What?" Doug asked, trying to read his face.

"I think this might be what we need," Earl said.

"But we can't read any of it, it's all gobbledygook!"

Earl shut the book and tucked it under one arm. "Look, we'll take it to the library. That old lady might know where we could get some kind of book to help us. Then we can look up each word, one at a time, like a decoder ring."

Doug thought for a second before saying, "But then she'll ask where you got the book! What will we say?"

Earl shook his head. "I'll write the words down, as best as I can get them. I'll say it's for a project. Plus, everyone knows us as the orphans now—they all feel sorry for us. No one'll bother about us wanting something from the library."

Doug nodded in grim resolution. "Alright, but leave that thing in the barn. It gives me the creeps."

Earl nodded and took one last look at the words on the page before closing the book and sliding it under some straw in the loft. When he did, the wind immediately stopped blowing around them.

The boys exchanged a worried glance before climbing down from the loft and sneaking back inside the house.

* * *

They had converted the Cabin Creek Public Library from an old log cabin, one of the original buildings from when the town was first founded in 1801. There were just a few dozen rows of books, and more than one town resident thought the term "library" was generous for the small building. The cousins walked there after school the following day. Both boys stopped at the door before entering, and Earl fidgeted with the scrap of paper in his pocket.

Doug looked at him. "What's wrong?"

"Nothin," Earl lied. His stomach had been in knots since they left the barn. The way the wind had blown around them, as if to open the book to the page with the man laying down, had filled him with a dread that was unlike anything he had ever experienced.

Carmine Mortem Ut Inmortui

He continued to thumb the piece of paper with the strange words on it as they walked into the library.

Marylou Betenner was at the desk, chewing gum loudly while thumbing through a worn copy of *Tom Sawyer*. She raised her eyebrows when the boys walked in, eyeing the sad-looking pair in front of her.

"C'n I help y'all?"

Earl nodded and stepped forward, handing her a piece of paper. "We'd like a decoder for this, Ma'am."

She picked up the piece of paper and looked down the bridge of her nose over her glasses. "A decoder?" she giggled. "Y'all mean a translator? This is in Latin. What are ya, Catholic?"

The boys looked at each other and then back at her, shaking their heads. "No, Ma'am, it's for a school project."

She studied them for a moment, drumming her hands on the table. Finally, she nodded and smiled warmly. "Alright, let me get you a Latin dictionary. Y'all are lucky. We only have a couple of language dictionaries, Latin and French, and the French one's missin' anyhow…" she said, trailing off as she walked away.

The boys fidgeted as they waited, shifting their weight nervously from foot to foot. Both of their hearts were beating quickly, and even though they were simply asking a librarian for a dictionary, it somehow seemed that they were doing something wrong. Maybe even sinister.

Finally, Marylou came back with a thick, dusty-looking book and set it on the table with a thud. "Now, boys, this is a reference book, so it's not for circulation. That means you'll have to look at it here, and you can't take it home."

The boys nodded and Earl reached up to pick up the book and take it to the small table in the library's corner. "We won't. Thank you, Miss Marylou."

The librarian smiled over her horn-rimmed glasses as she watched the boys walk away with the dictionary. She furrowed her brow for a moment, thinking of the awful things she'd heard about their mothers. Marylou would never admit it aloud, but a thought entered her mind as the little orphan boys sat down with the worn old book: she wondered if the boys weren't better off without those women. Shaking her head, slightly embarrassed at having such a thought, she went back to reading *Tom Sawyer* for the fortieth time.

* * *

That night, Earl and Doug lay in the little twin beds their cousin's wife had made up for them in the guest room. Each stared up at the ceiling with wide eyes, thinking about the things they had discovered at the library. Neither of them had spoken for a long while after that. They walked back to their cousin's house silently, only speaking to say "Thank you, Ma'am" and "Yes, sir" at dinner.

Finally, Doug broke the silence. "You think our moms were really… I mean—"

"Witches," Earl said, uttering the dreaded word. "Yeah, I do."

Doug furrowed his brow and turned to face Earl, leaning up on one elbow. "They were always nice to us."

"Of course they were. Just 'cause we know what they were now, that doesn't change nothin' about them being our moms. They were good at that, and that's all I need to know," Earl said.

"Death Spell for the Undead. Make Him Rest. I can't get it out of my head... are you sure that's what it said?"

"You were there with me, Doug. It was all there in the dictionary. Momma wanted me—wanted *us*—to see it. To make him rest."

"Maybe that's how we keep him from hurting anyone again."

Earl sat silently for a moment. "Maybe. But I was thinking..."

"What?" Doug whispered.

"Maybe Momma was wrong," Earl said.

Doug nodded in the dark. "They shouldn't have been fooling around with all this. It never would have started."

"That's not what I mean, Doug. I mean, maybe Harvey don't *need* rest," Earl said.

"Huh?" Doug asked.

Earl continued, "Maybe he don't *deserve* rest. Why should Harvey get to rest? He was a lousy sonofabitch—a woman beater when he was alive, a murderer, now he's dead."

"But he could hurt other people."

"What if we made sure he didn't?"

"How?"

"Feed him, maybe."

"Earl!" Doug whispered loudly.

"Just petty stuff, I mean. Squirrels, mice. Just enough to keep him alive. Keep him suffering. Like a zombie, like in the movies," Earl said.

"For how long?"

"Forever."

Doug rolled over to lie on his back again. Even though he couldn't see Earl in the dark, he didn't want to face him in this moment. For the first time, he was afraid of his cousin.

But Earl had decided. He had answered the call.

"Tomorrow night," he said, "We'll head down to the cemetery and pay our pal Harvey a little visit."

* * *

The boys rode their bikes down State Road 39 in the dark, their path illuminated only by the white light of a waning September moon. The road was lined with old railroad ties and trees that hung heavy with rust-colored leaves, barely visible in the dark. A chorus of cicadas played their anthem, which was the only sound other than the wheels of their bicycles whizzing down the road.

The pair didn't speak. Earl rode in front and Doug in back, and after a silent fifteen miles, Earl pulled to the right to park. The boys leaned their bikes up against a tree on the other side of the ties lining the road. Earl took off the small backpack he was wearing, pulled out a flashlight, and turned it on.

In front of them was the head of a path leading to the cemetery. It was narrow but well-trod, and between the flashlight and the moonlight, they'd be able to see where they were heading. For a second, the boys just stood there at the mouth of the trail, until Doug spoke up.

"Let's go."

Earl, startled, turned to look at him. He couldn't quite tell in the dark, but it looked like Doug was crying. Earl reached a hand out and touched his shoulder. "We're gonna get him."

Doug turned away, wiping his face with one sleeve. Then, without another word, the boys stepped onto the trail.

The moon seemed to grow brighter as the boys neared their destination. As they walked, the leaves crunched under their feet and the cicadas grew louder. The year's first cool autumn breeze whipped around them.

Earl stopped in front of Doug and shone the flashlight, illuminating a small old cemetery with a wrought-iron gate and a faded sign.

"CABIN CREEK CEMETERY EST. 1801"

The boys' heart rates increased as they crossed through the gate into the graveyard. The headstones were in fairly good shape considering their age, and the pair made their way towards the back corner on the western side of the cemetery, where the newer graves were.

They walked on, careful not to step on or trip over any stones. Whatever their mothers had been in life, they had at least taught the boys their manners, and both knew it was disrespectful, not to mention bad luck, to step on a grave. Finally, they came to the spot they had been searching for. A stone lay crooked on the ground, near a pile of loose earth.

"Harvey Ward
b. 1910 d. 1959
Turn, mortal, turn, thy dangers know,
Where'r thy foot can tread;
The earth rings hollow from below,
And warns thee by her dead."

Earl shone the flashlight on the words when a sound came from somewhere behind them. The boys whipped around, coming face to face with a dirt-caked Harvey, still wearing the brown suit Nadine had him buried in.

"Earl..." Doug said, his voice shaking.

Without a word, Earl slipped the bag off of his shoulders. He reached a hand inside and pulled out a smaller plastic bag, then dumped the contents on the ground between himself and what remained of Harvey.

"Here you go, you lousy bastard."

Harvey's eyes went wide, and he dove to the ground, picking up the dead squirrel that had fallen out. Snarling, he ate it.

"Oh, Jesus," Doug whispered. "This can't be real—"

"It's real, alright." A smile had crept across Earl's face.

Doug turned to look at his cousin. In the pale moonlight, he could see that Earl was proud of what he'd done. Doug's face curled in disgust as the sounds of Harvey chewing filled his ears. "This is wrong, Earl. No matter what he done, this is wrong!"

Earl kept his eyes on Harvey. He wasn't sure what he was feeling, but it was something like satisfaction. Somehow, this was perfect, despite the nagging voice in his head warning that he had crossed a line. "Says who?" he demanded.

"*I* do! You can't keep him like a pet—this is torture!" Doug cried.

"He ain't a pet, Doug," Earl said, raising both hands to shove his cousin backwards.

Doug stumbled back a few steps and looked at Earl in shock, then swallowed hard.

"Oh yeah? How are you going to keep this up?" he asked.

Earl shrugged and turned back to Harvey. He reached into the bag and picked up a chipmunk, tossing it at Harvey as if he was throwing bread crumbs at a flock of pigeons.

"Keep comin' out here. Bring him small stuff like this. As long as I can. As long as it takes."

Doug's mouth hung open as he looked at Earl, then at Harvey. "I'm going back. I don't want no part of this—"

Earl got close to Doug, gripping his shirt with both hands. "It's too late for that, Doug. We're all we've got now. And whose fault is that? He made *orphans* of us, Doug. Orphans!" he cried, gesturing at Harvey, who was now gnawing on the tail of the chipmunk.

Doug studied what used to be a man for a minute without speaking. Finally, he nodded dimly, and Earl released his grip on him.

"You don't have to come out with me every night, but you're sure as hell going to keep this secret, Doug. Aren't you? Aren't you!" Earl demanded.

Doug looked at Earl with tears of anger in his eyes. He nodded again, and Earl slipped an arm around his shoulder. They watched Harvey finish, after which he seemed to settle back into a sleep-like state under a tree near his grave. The book had said that would happen. The creature wouldn't be up again until dusk the next day. Earl smiled again. For the time being, at least Harvey was resting.

The boys rode their bikes back in silence, now joined by a bond of secrets as well as blood.

* * *

Earl drummed his fingers on his desk as that night replayed in his head for the ten millionth time. He leaned back and looked out his office window once more, wondering what to do about his cousin's little problem.

If the cows were missing, it was simply a matter of volume. Their old friend Harvey clearly needed more food. Something bigger. That wasn't in the old book, but he supposed it was possible that, over time, Harvey's need for food might increase. The Sheriff pursed his lips together and sighed. Then he stood up, stretched, and grabbed the ring of keys off of his desk.

His boots clicked as he left his office and walked down the hall to the jailhouse holding cell. A hitchhiker—some long-haired hippie he had arrested the previous day for loitering outside the town diner off of the highway—sat on a cot behind a row of bars. The hippie stood and looked hopeful as the Sheriff walked up the cell and grinned, placing the key in the lock.

You'll do. You'll do just fine, Earl thought, unlocking the cell door.

"Really, I can go now?" the young man asked as the cell door slid open.

The Sheriff nodded. "Sure can, seems that this was all a big misunderstanding. You're free as a bird."

The young man stepped out of the cell and stretched, looking around. "Thank you, Sheriff. Say, I don't suppose I could get a ride back to the highway? Wouldn't want to get picked up for loitering again," he said with a smile.

Earl laughed and slapped the kid on the back, leading him back down the hallway to the front of the station.

"Son," the Sheriff grinned, "It's your lucky day."

THE DEVIL YOU KNOW

"It comes from everywhere and nowhere and dies away at dawn," she hissed in a thick Spanish accent.

A fluorescent light buzzed above them, illuminating the small examination room in an unnatural yellow glow. The patient and her doctor sat across from one other at the table, a thin layer of plexiglass between them with a square shaped hole at the bottom for medications to be passed back and forth. The woman quickly reached her hand through the slot and dropped something small into the doctor's coffee as he read from his notes.

Dr. Martell looked up, startled at her words. He had just reviewed the patient's file and had not yet asked her questions.

"What does?" he asked, taking a sip from the cup, wincing as he choked it down. *Even shittier than usual*, he thought.

The woman had black, scraggly hair and wore a hospital-issued gown. She looked around as if to make sure no one was listening, then leaned in towards the screen. Her hands were flat on the table and her head was down when she opened her mouth to answer.

"The devils. The sounds they make at night," she said. She looked up and leaned toward the plexiglass screen, her breath fogging it. The woman broke into a crooked, insane smile. "I've heard them. And soon, you will, too."

The doctor kept his eyes locked on hers, concealing any reaction to what she was saying. This was less than an arduous task because the patient was spouting utter nonsense. She heard devils at night—sure. This was the same woman who, when first admitted to the asylum, tried to convince a team of nurses that she was four-hundred and seven years old. Arlene Espoza was, in layman's terms, a loon.

Still, the doctor had a job to do. He looked once more at her file, giving it a cursory glance, before continuing. "Do you know why you're here, Mrs. Espoza?"

She sat silently, staring at the ground. He waited for an answer, and the moment seemed to drag on, the buzzing of the light fixture above them growing louder. The doctor leaned forward slightly.

"Can you hear me?" he asked, taking another sip of coffee. He winced again as it slid bitterly down his throat.

Suddenly, the patient whipped her head up, reached a hand into her hair, and pulled a giant chunk of it out of her scalp. Without looking at the clump of hair, she slammed it down on the table.

Dr. Martell, only barely shocked by this display, motioned towards a pair of burly orderlies in the corner who quickly approached Arlene and wrapped her back into a straightjacket, taking care to tie the belts securely. As they dragged her out of the room, the doctor saw Arlene mouth something at him.

"Soon."

He watched over his glasses until she was gone, then pushed them higher on the bridge of his nose before finishing his case notes. Arlene was the last patient of the day, and he was relieved he could now go home and work on his research. Dr. Martell closed the file and added it to the stack on the table, bound them all with a large rubber band, then stood up to leave the examination room.

On his way out of the building, the doctor walked down a long hall lined with cells on either side. This was the part of the hospital which housed the most ill patients, those for whom recovery was less of a focus than was maintenance. They heavily sedated most of them to keep them from harming themselves or the medical staff. Each of the patients in this part of the institution had been on a steady diet of Droxetine since before they entered the hospital, and Dr. Martell h tasked with observing the effects of the drug.

There was Rose Young, a young mother who had drowned all four of her children in the bathtub because voices told her it was the only way to save them. On her left was Luis Daley, a man with the most severe case of obsessive-compulsive disorder he had ever seen, who was counting the tiles in his cell for probably the billionth time. He was completely bald. Luis had spent the previous years pulling out his hair one strand at a time, out of fear that there were an uneven number of them on his head.

Barbara Qualls occupied the last cell on the right. She was laying in bed in a state that was officially called sleep but in reality was more like a medically induced coma. They kept her sedated so that she would stop slamming her head against the walls, her bed, the toilet—anything within reach. Finally, Arlene was last on the left, and she sat cross-legged on the floor, watching Dr. Martell as he walked down the hall. She mouthed the word again through the glass.

"Soon."

He ignored her. Dr. Martell had learned it was best not to give them attention and, if he was completely honest, he simply didn't care. He turned the key to unlock the door and then locked it again behind him.

His mind was already on that evening's work as he walked out of the hospital lobby into the parking garage. Dr. Martell whistled a song as he fished his car keys out of his briefcase and walked through the dark. He approached his brand new Corvette and looked twice when he thought he saw a shadow duck out from behind one of the concrete barriers.

"Hello?" he said to the darkness. When no one answered, he shrugged and got into the car.

It was only a fifteen minute drive from the hospital to his luxury condo on the other side of town. As part of the divorce settlement, his wife had received their primary residence, a sprawling estate on a nearby lake, so this condo was home for the foreseeable future. It only had one bedroom, but his children hadn't spoken to him since the affair, so he had no reason to make room for visitors.

Their loss.

Dr. Martell parked in the gated resident's lot next to the condo building and gathered his files before stepping out into the rainy city streets. He yawned, suddenly tired, as he walked to the elevator of his building and gave a polite nod to the operator.

"Good evening doctor," the young man said as he pressed the button for the top floor penthouse suite.

"Evening, Hector," Dr. Martell replied, stepping inside.

"Don't you want to hold the door for your friend?" Hector asked, putting one hand against the elevator door to pause it.

The doctor was already reviewing a file he held open in his hands and looked up in annoyance at the still-open door. "I'm sorry?"

"Your friend? I saw you walking with someone outside the building, but they stopped when you entered. It looked like they were waiting for you to let them in."

Dr. Martell shook his head and yawned again. "No visitors tonight, Hector." He eyed the door impatiently.

Hector looked towards the building lobby and then back at the doctor before nodding and letting go of the door. "My mistake. Good evening, Sir," he said. The doorman smiled, but his eyes wore a look of concern.

Dr. Martell grunted and looked back down at his file as the elevator closed and began its rise. He was so engrossed in reading that he barely heard the ding of the doors sliding open.

The elevator led directly into his suite and its bird's-eye view of the city. The rain hadn't let up yet, and it splashed against the floor-to-ceiling windows, blotting the normally breathtaking view with a watery curtain. Dr. Martell put his keys in a ceramic dish by the front door and walked straight to the office in the back corner of the penthouse.

Still not looking up, he pulled a leather executive chair out from behind his desk and sat down. Thunder cracked outside, and he jumped, suddenly aware of the severity of the storm. One wall of the home office comprised floor-to-ceiling windows, and for a moment, Dr. Martell simply sat and stared out at the view. Storm clouds swirled in the sky like great waves. He turned back to the desk and jumped.

A figure had just peeked around the door of his office. The doctor blinked hard twice.

My eyes are tired.

He suppressed any other thought and went back to his work. In his experience, there was always an explanation, and, if not, a pill that could solve the problem. He reached up to pull the string on his lamp and it turned on with a click.

A dark figure flashed again in the doorway, then disappeared. Dr. Martell inhaled sharply and furrowed his brow. Chewing on the inside of one lip, he turned his eyes back to his work.

His research was an evaluation of sorts, a case study on the effects of Droxetine in patients suffering from paranoid schizophrenia. His position was that, despite its harsh physical side effects, it should be promoted among psychiatric patients and even tested on patients with milder diagnoses such as obsessive-compulsive disorder, severe phobias, and even generalized anxiety and panic disorders. That's where Arlene, Luis, Rose, and Barbara came in. They had been taking the drug for years. First, as his patients who had mild psychiatric problems, then the treatment continued after they were committed to the hospital, even as their mental health deteriorated further into more severe psychoses.

The problem he now faced was deemphasizing mounting evidence that, while some patients' symptoms improved, a significant minority of patients who took Droxetine for ten months or longer worsened. Significantly.

One such patient was Arlene Espoza. She had arrived at the facility after taking the drug for six months, and they had continued to administer it despite her resistance. When first taken, it had a mild sedative effect, which helped the nurses put her and all the other Droxetine patients back in their cells and bought them a few hours of quiet. It was after a few months that around ten percent of patients suffered hallucinations and paranoia. Once, a nurse had remarked that it hardly seemed worth it, considering how some patients declined severely after administering the drug. Dr. Martell's response had startled her.

"Better the devil you know than the devil you don't."

He leaned back from his laptop and put both hands behind his head, chewing on a pen, and thought of their meeting earlier this morning. He wasn't invested in Mrs. Espoza as a patient. Rather, he observed her the way a tenth grader would a frog being dissected in biology class. After all, the doctor had been prescribing Droxetine for a few years now, and only these four patients seemed to suffer any severe effects. Out of his forty patients, only these four had lost everything. The unlucky ten percent.

Dr. Martell went back to his laptop and began to type. *Patient E shows a significant improvement.* A lie. Arlene was crazier than ever. But, he had received a tip that if his paper was supportive of Droxetine he may have a generous supporter of future research endeavors in the pharmaceutical company who manufactured the drug.

He yawned for the third time since he entered the building and looked at the clock. It was only half past seven in the evening, but he was as drowsy as if it were well past midnight. The doctor tried to concentrate on the patient files from earlier and leaned one hand on his head. His vision was blurry, and it was becoming hard to concentrate. A thought struck him, and he bolted upright in his chair.

Drugged. I've been drugged!

He took his glasses off and rubbed his face with both hands, trying to steady his mind.

But how? Who?

He thought once more of his last patient of the day and of the bitter cup of coffee.

Arlene.

Dr. Martell got up from his desk and staggered to the kitchen, reaching for the phone on the counter. He picked it up before a word replayed in his head—the same one Arlene had uttered as he walked past her glass cell door earlier that evening.

"Soon."

* * *

Dr. Martell was falling.

He was screaming, too, as he fell. It was as if he had slipped into a black hole. Hot, dark walls surrounded him on all sides. His arms were wrapped around his torso, and he looked down to see that, to his horror, he was fully strapped into a straightjacket. The doctor tilted his head back and screamed even louder. For what felt like an eternity, he continued to fall down a dark, narrow tunnel.

As he fell further, the doctor felt sharp, bony hands reaching out to grab him. They clawed at the straight jacket and pulled at his hair, and their *screams*—he had never heard anything so horrible. They were the cries of a million souls damned to Hell.

I'm insane, he thought as he fell.

Dr. Martell stopped screaming and let the madness slip over him, weeping silently.

* * *

After what seemed like an eternity, he woke up on the kitchen floor. His head was throbbing, and he reached up to touch a tender spot on his temple that had collided with the counter when he passed out.

He sucked a giant breath in and then coughed it out.

A dream. A horrible dream. That's all!

His vision was doubled, reminding him he had been drugged. The doctor struggled to sit up, leaning with his back against the counter.

Arlene. She slipped me the pill. Of course she did. She's bat shit insane. But, oh God, the side effects.

He thought of how horribly he had suffered from one dosage—assuming she had only given him one dosage—and considered then the patients that had been taking them daily for years, some twice a day. He winced, suddenly awash in shame and regret, when a shadow darted out from his bedroom and across the hall to the bathroom.

The doctor's face twisted in fear and he called out in a trembling voice, "Who's there?"

All thoughts of Arlene were erased from his mind. Someone was in his home.

Against his better judgment, the doctor ran into the bathroom and turned the lights on. Finding no one, he opened the bathroom closet. Still nothing. He reached a hand up to run through his hair and sat down on the edge of the enormous tub.

He tried to remember how long the side effects of a single dose of Droxetine would last, but his thoughts were still cloudy. He heard a noise and snapped his head up just in time to see a shadowy figure dart again from the doorway of the bathroom.

Dr. Martell stood up and shouted, "Who's there? Goddamnit, I'm calling the police!"

He charged groggily out of the bathroom and headed again towards the phone on the kitchen counter. Dialing rapidly, thanking a God he didn't believe in that he had kept the landline telephone when he bought the penthouse, he tried to imagine what he would say, when a voice growled in his ear.

"Put the phone down," it demanded.

Dr. Martell jumped and turned around. No one was there.

"Hang up the phone." The voice was deep and menacing.

He whipped around again to see where it was coming from and found no one. Dr. Martell slid a kitchen drawer open and reached for a meat cleaver.

"Hit yourself in the head. Use the mallet," the voice said.

Dr. Martell dropped the tool back into the drawer. "No!" he screamed, looking up and around to find the source of the voice.

The doctor opened the fridge and grabbed an opened bottle of white wine, which he grabbed and drank from greedily, desperate for something, anything, to numb the terror. His eyes watered as it went down, and he turned towards the floor to ceiling windows.

Walking over to them, he put one hand on the glass and stared down the twelve stories to the earth below. For a minute, he calmed a little, just listening to the rain rap against the glass. Then the voice came again.

"Throw yourself out the window. If you get a running start, the glass will break. Take a few steps back and throw yourself against it, you'll see."

Dr. Martell groaned in frustration and despair.

"Do it!" the voice howled.

His stomach churned as he realized with horror that the voice was coming from within his mind. A question, clear and concise, emerged from the logical part of his brain.

If a patient told you they were hearing voices when no one was around, what would you do?

The doctor was awash in shame. He knew exactly what he'd do for them. He would prescribe them twenty milligrams daily of Droxetine. If they were already taking the drug, he would recommend an increase in their dosage.

He fainted again.

* * *

Dr. Martell woke up on the floor in front of his couch as the sun rose, trying to remember if the previous evening had all been some kind of hellish, stress-induced nightmare. But, his head was throbbing as if he had a hangover, which told him that the Droxetine was finally wearing off. It had been real.

Arlene.

Dr. Martell stood up and ran to the door, stopping only to grab his wallet and put on some shoes. He pressed the button for the lobby and eyed the plastic buttons impatiently as the elevator made its slow crawl downstairs.

"Morning, Doctor!" Hector smiled as the doors opened to the first floor.

The doctor ignored him and bolted out of the elevator. He had to get back to the asylum, and he had to do it quickly, before they administered the medicine for the day. The tires of his car squealed as he pulled frantically out of the parking garage and sped off in the asylum's direction. On the short drive there, he thought of Arlene's words from yesterday.

"It comes from everywhere and nowhere and dies away at dawn."

"The devils. The sounds they make at night. I've heard them. And soon, you will, too."

The doctor pulled haphazardly into his parking space at the hospital, putting a dent in the Corvette. Not stopping to lock the car, he bolted from his car to the automatic front doors of the institution. He practically threw his ID badge at the nurse at the front desk.

"Everything okay, Doctor?" she shouted as he ignored her and scurried by.

Dr. Martell burst through the double doors of Arlene's wing and stood, panting, at the head of the hallway. What he saw stopped him from running immediately down the hall into her cell.

To his left, Rose, still a young woman of thirty-five, sat bedraggled on her cot. One of those things, the shadow figures, sat next to her, stroking her hair. It whispered things in her ear, but he could tell by its sneer and menacing scowl they were obscenities and lies. Rose nodded with dead eyes in response as it spoke.

The doctor took a few steps down the hall and looked to his right.

Luis Daley was wiping the glass wall of his cell frantically with a pillowcase. A shadowy creature was repeating something and pointing at different spots on the glass wall, and as he pointed, Luis frantically wiped the spot, then the next, in a never-ending cycle of cleaning. Sweat dripped from his forehead. He suddenly noticed Dr. Martell staring and stopped wiping for a second. Then the creature shrieked and pointed once more and Luis cried, picking up the pillowcase to wipe again at the glass.

The knot that had been growing in the doctor's stomach tightened and grew as he looked at Luis with pity. He took a shaky breath and began the long walk to Arlene's cell.

On his way there, he glanced at the last cell on the right. Barbara Qualls sat on the floor cross-legged, her head bandaged from the many times she had slammed it against the cell walls. Hers was the only padded cell. One of them, the creatures, was squatting in the corner, pointing and laughing at the bandages on her head, a horrible, deep laugh that made Dr. Martell feel deeply ill.

He ran down the hallway, finally stopping at Arlene's cell. She was lying curled up in the corner, looking tired and wounded. One of the shadow figures was crouched next to her, howling in her ear, its jagged teeth sticking out from its mouth. It screamed foul and insane things, and Arlene nodded weakly in response, her mouth agape.

Despite all of this, Dr. Martell saw, for the first time, the woman behind the matted black hair and straight jacket. Her eyes, though shiny with despair, were a brilliant blue. A pang of guilt that had started as a small twinge when he entered the hospital now throbbed within his guts. Dr. Martell raised a hand to the glass and choked back a sob.

Arlene noticed the doctor, got up from her cot, and walked towards him, her head held high. The figure stayed crouched in the corner, pawing one hand out as she walked by as if to scratch her with its long, jagged talons.

"I heard them. I can *see* them!" Dr. Martell yelled to her through the glass.

She raised one hand to touch where his was on the other side and nodded weakly, tears falling from her eyes as she smiled and shut them tightly against the whispering behind her.

When she opened them again, Dr. Martell was still standing there, and she knew by the look on his face that he really could see them, too. Despite the foul sounds coming from the thing in her cell, and the memory of the creature's hot, hateful breath in her ear, for the first time in many years, Arlene Espoza realized that someone believed her, and that things would finally change.

FLASHING LIGHTS

Hank Bowser was driving down a divided highway through the middle of nowhere, Ohio, when he came upon the outskirts of a town that looked like many others on his trips through the Midwest. The sign marking it said *"Welcome to Haverford,"* and to the left of that was his last delivery site of the trip—a McDonald's.

Hank smiled, pulling over to park. With a groan, he unbuckled his seatbelt and got out of the car, stretching his arms over his head to get the kinks out from the long drive. He hadn't stopped since somewhere back in New York. Exhausted, he let out an extended yawn as he stretched. Hank felt the first few drops of a spring rain fall on his head and rushed to the back of the truck to unload packages of frozen beef patties onto the dolly.

The salty-fat smell of the fryer hit his nose the second he opened the back door of the restaurant, and after he made sure the patties got to the right spot, he made his way to the store's front counter and ordered a quarter-pounder with cheese, large fries, and an extra-large Diet Coke. Waiting for his food, Hank looked out the rain-streaked windows at the town of Haverford. There was a hospital across the street, a gas station on the next corner, and not much else. He sighed, the familiar depression of endless, one-stoplight towns washing over him.

His order came up, and he carried it outside, grabbing the burger out of the paper bag and taking a bite as he climbed back into the truck. As he did, a pickle slid out of the burger and down the front of his jumpsuit. He ran a hand down to wipe it off, only dragging a smear of mustard across his name tag and buttons. Shrugging, he put the truck in drive and pulled out of the parking lot. As he pulled back out on to the road, he silently hoped he could find a nearby motel to hunker down in for the night. The rain was falling harder, and it did nothing to help his motivation to take the truck all the way back through Ohio to New York.

As he pulled out of the McDonald's, the road went slightly downhill before plateauing out into the heart of what looked like every other small town he drove through on these deliveries. The light turned green, and he pulled ahead, the highway rising to take him out of the small valley town, when a large building appeared behind a wall of oak trees. As he approached the next traffic light, he read the sign next to the building.

HAVERFORD COMMUNITY GENERAL HOSPITAL—

There were a few words after "Hospital," but the rain blurred them so that he could not tell what they were. More clouds rolled in as Hank grabbed a handful of fries and tossed them down his throat, followed by a large gulp of his drink. Reaching across the seat for some napkins in the glove compartment, he paused. A tall, blonde woman was rushing through the rain, speed-walking out of the hospital. She wore blue scrubs which were soaked through to where he could make out the lines of her undergarments.

Hank smiled and pulled up closer to the woman, rolling down the passenger side window. Lightning cracked, and the rain fell harder, so that he had to shout out the window to get her attention.

"Can I give you a ride, Ma'am?" he said, doing his best to smile handsomely. A gob of cheeseburger was stuck in his beard.

The woman wasn't carrying an umbrella, but held a clipboard above her head to block the rain. She furrowed her brow as she looked inside his truck, grinning tightly at Hank. "Well, I was just walking home, actually."

Hank caught sight of the cheeseburger in his beard in the rear-view mirror and wiped it away self-consciously. He cleared his throat. "Raining pretty hard. If you'd rather not walk, I don't mind dropping you off somewhere." He watched the woman eye him apprehensively in the rain. Thunder cracked again.

She looked from side to side, then turned around to look back at the hospital. Tilting her head at Hank, she said, "Well… if you're sure you don't mind?"

"Not at all."

Hank smiled and reached across to open the passenger side door, grabbing the grease-stained sack of food and tossing it into the backseat in one motion.

"Hop in."

The woman cast one more furtive glance at the hospital before hurrying into the van. Hank reached into the backseat and grabbed a grimy-looking towel, which he handed to her. She studied it for a minute before using it to wipe the rain off of her face and neck. Strands of blonde hair clung to her face as she turned her head to him. "Thanks. I'm Daisy, by the way," she said, reaching out a hand to shake.

"Hank. Where you headed?"

"I'm going home to my family. It's just on the outskirts of town," she said, buckling herself in and taking several deep breaths.

Hank leered at her for a moment before putting the car in drive and pulled back out onto the highway, but not before scanning her left hand for a ring. She wasn't wearing one, and he smiled to himself. "Pretty big hospital. You worked there long?" he asked.

"Hmm? Oh, no, not long," she replied, looking out the passenger window.

The highway began its incline and the lights of town grew dimmer as they drove away and the sky darkened above them. The pair rode in silence for a few moments before either spoke again.

"Just tell me where to turn next," Hank said.

Daisy turned around to look out the rear windshield and said, "It's up another few miles. You'll turn right on State Road 46."

Hank shifted his eyes to the right to look at Daisy as he drove. The woman hadn't turned away from the windows since she first got into his truck. In fact, she hadn't looked at him once. He turned to face the front windshield again and saw that the light ahead had turned red. Abruptly, Hank hit the brakes.

"Sorry."

She turned from the window for the first time, a serene look on her face. "Oh, it's no problem. Listen, I'm in quite a rush to see my family. Once we're off the main road here, do you mind speeding up a little?" She flashed a smile at Hank, and he nodded in return.

"Thanks," she said. "Hank?"

"Yes?" he asked, staring at her greedily.

She pointed out the front windshield and said, "The light's green."

He pressed the gas so quickly that the truck jumped and the tires squealed. "Sorry," he repeated.

"You can stop apologizing," she said.

He smiled shyly just as blue and red lights flashed in his rear-view mirror.

"Shit," he said. "Shit."

Daisy whipped her head around and took one look at the flashing lights in the rear-view mirror before pressing herself back against the passenger seat. Shutting her eyes tightly, she pulled both knees up to her chest. "That's them. Oh, God!"

"That's who? The cop? You know him?"

She looked at Hank in desperation. "They can't catch up with us, speed up," she said, her eyes frantic.

"What do you mean?" Hank said, studying her face, which was scrunched tight with fear. "You know the cop?"

She sunk down in the seat and unbuckled her safety belt. "You can't let them find me. They'll take me away from my family."

"Who is this guy? An ex-boyfriend or something?" Hank asked, still eyeing the lights as they got ever closer to the back of his truck. Both vehicles were approaching a fork on the divided highway.

Daisy looked up at him from the floor of the car. "They hurt me, they want to take me away from my family, you can't let them." She sat up and looked into the side mirror, then shot a desperate look at Hank. "Please, don't let them take me!"

Hank looked again at the lights flashing in the rear-view mirror, then to his right at the hysterical woman in his passenger seat. Her clothes, still soaking wet, clung to her attractive frame. They were a quarter of a mile from the fork in the road when he decided to do as she said, jerking the steering wheel violently to the right. The truck hydroplaned for a few feet and fishtailed before he gained control and they sped off into the right fork. The police car did not have enough time to merge, and as Hank craned his neck to the left, he saw the car slow down. He looked back over at Daisy, now breathing heavily.

"Did we lose them? Thank God!" she cried, jumping back into the seat and grabbing at the lapels of his jumpsuit.

Hank blushed and pushed the gas pedal harder. "Sure thing, but we'd better turn soon, or he's going to catch up with us," Hank said, scanning the road for an out.

Daisy sniffed and wiped her eyes with her hands, sitting back up as she buckled her seatbelt. "Up a mile past that silo," she pointed, "Take a right on county road 950. It's narrow but it will get us home without running into anyone else."

The sound of sirens in the distance grew louder, and the road was gradually becoming less paved and more muddy with the recent rain so that they were dragging tracks behind them that would be easy to follow. As they approached the county road, Hank was pleased to find it paved, making it harder for anyone to follow their tracks.

What am I doing? What am I thinking?

Just as the sirens were closing in on them, Hank turned abruptly onto County Road 950 and sped up.

"Ok," he said, looking over at Daisy, "Now where?" Hank was flushed and ignited with a kind of excitement as he studied her face.

"Left, here!" she pointed suddenly, and Hank snapped out of his admiring gaze to press the brakes just in time to turn left on to a dirt road carved into a cornfield.

The tires sank into the wet ground and the leaves on the cornstalks brushed against the sides of his truck, some sticking into the side mirror and under the windshield wipers as he barreled through the field. The sounds of sirens grew dimmer.

I did it. I really lost them.

A slow grin spread across his face. He had never been in a police chase before. Well, he had never been in any kind of chase before. Not a lot of opportunity for it in the frozen beef patty delivery game, he supposed.

Daisy heaved a sigh of relief. She looked over at Hank gratefully and said, "Thank you. Only a few miles now. Just follow this road, then you'll take another right and you'll see it. There's a long driveway leading to an old yellow farmhouse. They're expecting me."

Hank drove on with a smile as Daisy leaned over and rested her head on his shoulder. The corn whizzed pleasantly by them, thunking every once in a while as a cob fell off and hit the side of the truck. The rain had cleared, and the air was no longer thick with humidity. A small rainbow appeared over the horizon as the sun peeked out from behind the clouds. Daisy and Hank drove in silence for the next few miles, admiring the post-storm view and breathing sighs of relief like co-conspirators who had just gotten away with a bank robbery.

The road and rows of corn ended, and Daisy sat up suddenly.

"Here, turn right," she said, pointing.

Hank turned the wheel and pulled the van out onto another dirt road that was so narrow it was more like a path, and a long gravel driveway leading to a big yellow farmhouse came into view.

"We're here," Daisy said, smiling at him. Hank felt a rush of something that felt like butterflies as she grabbed his hand. "I want you to meet the family," she said.

Hank felt like he was floating through some kind of dream. He stared into Daisy's eyes as if in a trance and nodded dimly. Navigating the winding gravel driveway, he pulled the truck up to the house and put it in park.

The yellow farmhouse had a wide porch with dozens of pots containing dead plants littered about. The grass was patchy and yellow. A screen door swung lazily in the breeze. Something in Hank's stomach flipped, and he paused just as he was about to unbuckle his seatbelt.

Daisy turned to him and grabbed both of his hands as his eyes were locked on the old house. She kissed him on the cheek, and said, "Hank, I can't wait for them to meet you. Thank you for everything." She flew out of the car and ran up to the porch. "I'm home!" she cried, running with both hands in the air.

Hank studied her for a moment, sitting in the car with his seat still buckled. Something inside him was screaming at him to stay put, and, without understanding why, he pushed the button that locked all the doors of the truck, swallowing hard.

As Daisy ran screaming towards the porch, the screen door opened, and dozens of people filed out. They were dressed similarly in white linen pants and matching shirts, and some held thick books in their hands. Daisy ran up to a man in the center of the group. He was taller than the rest of them and had a long beard. The man wore no shoes, and the others seemed to clamor around him. She leapt into his arms and hugged him. The man hugged her back at first, then pushed her away, holding her at arm's length as if to study her. He smiled as he did, but something about the dull look in his eyes chilled Hank's blood.

He watched as Daisy and the bearded man exchanged a few words. The other people had crowded around them, not saying a word, only watching.

Then, slowly, Daisy, the bearded man, and all the people in white linens turned their heads in unison to stare at Hank in the truck.

He inhaled sharply, the blood rushing to his face as his stomach turned. For a moment he was frozen, too afraid to do what something instinctual within himself was commanding: to move, to put the truck in reverse, to back out of there and forget about Daisy and the police chase and the whole insane ordeal.

While he sat frozen, the people in white approached his car calmly. The first one to reach the truck put one hand out and placed it on the hood, and the others followed suit until their hands were covering the outside of the vehicle.

Their eyes—my God—their eyes! he thought as they crowded around the truck, surrounding him on all sides. None of them were blinking. Their faces were drawn in tight grins which, frozen, spread unnaturally wide across their faces.

Hank snapped out of the momentary shock and jerked the truck into reverse, not caring whether he hit any of them. The truck backed up wildly, and several of the people fell as they tried to grab for it. Hank put the car in drive and sped back down the dirt path, up the county roads, and through the fields of corn to the highway. He became ill as he drove, and some of the cheeseburger from earlier were now on the front of his jumpsuit. Hanks wiped his face and clothes with the grimy towel that was still on the front seat.

He drove on for what seemed like a few hours, heading west on the same divided highway that had brought him to the little town of Haverford, and to Daisy. For a while, he could not form coherent thoughts. Eventually, his mind cleared, and he was left with a sense of unreality.

What the hell was that?

Hank exhaled loudly and whistled, then reached for the knob to start the radio, his hands shaking. He flitted through some stations that were mostly static, frustrated at the lack of a signal, desperate for something to get his mind off of what had just happened. The road was unfamiliar, the flat terrain somehow sinister in the waning hours of day.

I'm driving through the ass end of nowhere, he thought, a creeping sense of isolation washing over him. Finally, he found a country radio station which was playing an old Hank Williams song. To calm his nerves, Hank hummed along to *"I'm So Lonesome I Could Cry"* as the delivery truck charged down the highway.

It rained again, and a sudden bolt of lightning caused him to jerk, slipping the wheel slightly out of his hands. He over-corrected it and fishtailed on the empty highway for a few moments, then regained control of the truck. As he was catching his breath for the second time that day, a motel appeared ahead on the horizon. Next to it was a truck stop and a Dairy Mart. He breathed a small sigh of relief and decided to stop for the night and head back out early the next day.

New York could wait until morning while he gathered his wits.

* * *

Hank checked in to the Cloverleaf Motel with a box of truck station pizza and a six-pack from the Dairy Mart under one arm. The neon sign outside buzzed so loudly he could hear it even inside at the front desk. A woman of around four hundred pounds tossed him a single key and took his cash with nicotine-stained fingers, and Hank began the solitary walk to his room.

The numbers were falling off of the room's door, but he didn't care. Hank turned the key and walked in, tossing his overnight bag on the bed. He set the pizza box down on a table no bigger than a school kid's desk before stretching and looking around the room. There were holes in the brown carpet which exposed the cheap linoleum underneath. A strip of flypaper hung from the ceiling by the bathroom door. Hank grunted. He had seen worse motel rooms.

He turned on the tv, grabbed a slice of pizza and a can of beer and plopped down on the edge of the bed. Immediately, the nightly news flashed on the screen, illuminating his face in the dim room.

"We're coming to you live from WLTV News with an urgent report that a dangerous member of the Canopy of Light cult has escaped from Haverford Community General Hospital for the Criminally Insane—"

A picture flashed on the screen of an attractive blonde woman. A picture of Daisy.

"—considered extremely dangerous, authorities believe she and other members of the cult are responsible for the recent string of abductions and murders along State Road 46 outside Haverford.

We're asking for anyone with any information on her whereabouts to contact the task force at this number…"

The words rang in Hank's ear as he sat, dumbfounded, on the edge of the motel bed. The sounds of sirens soon replaced them.

For the second time that day, red and blue lights startled Hank, this time flashing dully behind the cheerless curtains of his motel room.

THE PUMPKIN PATCH

Camp would've been better than this, Cassie thought as she dragged a wheelbarrow across the yard towards where the pumpkins grew. It had been a cloudy couple of weeks, and today it seemed as if the sun would never poke through again.

After being expelled from school the previous spring, her parents had given her two options for the months until the fall semester started in late September: a special "refinement camp" for girls, or a few months of manual labor at her aunt's hobby farm. Reluctantly, she had chosen the latter.

The summer had been unseasonably cool. Now, in the waning days of September, the previous night brought the year's first hard frost. Today, a fog had settled over the small farm, casting a soft, grey blanket over the ground. A few yards down from Cassie, her cousin Sam was pulling a Radio Flyer wagon across the field behind the house, and little chips of red paint cracked and fell off as he navigated the bumps and rocks of the expansive backyard garden.

His mom had planted rows of corn at the front of the property, but they already harvested those. The garden the cousins were headed towards now was set far back on the land. Sam and Cassie wore identical grim looks as they made their way towards it. They walked through rows of wilted brown corn stalks, under a trellis with the withered remnants of green beans climbing its wires, and finally came to a stop in front of the biggest garden on the small farm: the pumpkin patch.

Large, round pumpkins littered the ground, ripe for the picking. Sam pulled the wagon in front of him and took the shovel out of it, speaking the first words either of them had shared in days. "I'll take these larger ones. You go over there and collect the smaller ones." He pointed to the right of the pumpkin patch where a warted collection of green, yellow, orange, and white pumpkins sprouted from the cracked, brown earth.

"Fine," Cassie replied.

Sam watched her sulk all the way over and bend down to collect the tiny gourds. He sneered as his cousin picked them up with her smooth hands and wiped the dirt off onto her jeans, which were torn neatly at the knees and had rhinestones on the back pockets. Rolling his eyes, he turned back to the wagon, where he picked up the large shovel to remove the ripe pumpkins from their vines. These were Connecticut Field Pumpkins, an heirloom seed variety Sam's mom planted because they produce pumpkins with the classic 'Jack 'O Lantern' look for which the people who stopped at their roadside stand happily paid five dollars a pound.

The vines connecting the pumpkins to the earth were so thick that Sam couldn't simply pluck the fruit from the vine—he had to hack at them with the pointed part of the shovel to cut them loose. Gripping it over his head with both hands, he aimed for the vine on the biggest pumpkin in the patch and brought the shovel down with all of his strength. It made a clean cut and landed with a clang against a rock in the soil. Sam bent down and picked up the pumpkin to put it in his wagon.

Cassie heard the clank of the metal shovel hitting rock and looked up from collecting gourds. Her eyes widened slightly as she watched her cousin lift the huge pumpkin up and put it in the wagon. She looked back down at the small collection of gourds sticking out of the ground at her feet. None of them were more than a few pounds, and they ranged in color from ivory to orange to deep green. Some had big lumps and were lopsided, others were tiny and round. There were also a few miniature white pumpkins scattered for effect. She bent down and plucked them one by one from their vines. The small wheelbarrow her aunt had given her for harvesting them was quickly full, and she stood up to bring the haul back around to the front of the house.

Sam hauled the Radio Flyer wagon as Cassie followed him out to the front yard. A few cars had pulled off to the side of the road and suburban families were climbing out of them towards the harvest cart. A large sign stood in front of it, signaling the spot for people who liked to use this time of year to take languorous drives into the countryside and admire the quaint farmhouses dotting the fields. Sam's mom, Martha, had made the sign marking the farm stand from an old wooden palette she sprayed white and then traced in large black letters.

HAND-PICKED HARVEST
PUMPKINS $5/LB
GOURDS $2 EACH

Sam approached the cart, and Cassie followed behind at a distance. They could hear the conversation Sam's mom was having with a woman in a yellow silk scarf.

"You know these are twenty-five cents a pound at the grocer's, right?" the woman asked. She was holding two dog leashes, each attached to overly groomed, large white poodles. Her husband was in the driver's seat of the Mercedes on the side of the road, where he kept the engine running.

Martha smiled widely, her red curls swept up in a ponytail at the top of her head. "You are more than welcome to buy them from the grocer."

Scoffing, the woman set the gourds down on the cart before yanking the leashes and walking with her dogs back to the Mercedes.

"Nice, Mom," Sam laughed as he began unloading the pumpkins into barrels next to the cart.

"Well," she said, rolling up the sleeves of her plaid work shirt, "If we don't sell them, they make nice decorations, anyhow. " She brushed a strand of brown curls out of her son's face. "Where's Cassie?"

"I'm coming," a voice came from behind them. Cassie hoisted the basket of gourds up onto the cart and took them out one by one.

Martha looked proudly at her niece. "How's the fresh air treating you?"

Cassie shrugged and pushed her lips out. "Alright, I guess. It's not like it's smoggy at home or anything, not like the movies. It's a clean city."

She nudged her niece. "I'm teasing you, kid. Sam, have you checked the chickens yet?"

He rolled his eyes. "Not since this morning. They haven't been laying right for weeks."

Martha put her hands on her hips and furrowed her brow as she looked back towards the chicken coop in the back end of their property. She took a deep breath, looking at the sunset, and clapped her hands together. "Well! I think it's about time we pack it in for the day. What's the crew think?"

The kids nodded, and Martha picked the cash box up off the cart. "How does some hot cider sound?" she asked, putting her arms around both of them and leading them towards the house.

Sam and his mom made small talk as they walked down the mile-long driveway, and Cassie let her mind wander towards home. Though she missed the city, she liked that at Sam's, there were so many trees that the cold fall wind was blocked mostly. The downside was that she couldn't see the sky at night, since the heaps of leaves and branches only allowed small splinters of moonlight to slip through the trees. It was like being under a jungle canopy, only in the middle of Iowa. As her mind drifted towards home, she glanced up at the house.

A silhouette stood in the window of the upstairs guest room, where Cassie slept. The figure was glowing white and opaque and stood facing her. Its hands were against the windows, banging on them. Cassie stopped in her tracks, squinted, and stared at it closely. The figure opened its jaw and let out a howling scream.

Instinctively, Cassie covered her ears and knelt to the ground. Sam and Martha stopped in their tracks and looked back.

"Cassie? Cass, what is it?" Martha asked, concerned. She rushed back to her niece and knelt down next to her.

Cassie looked up, removing her hands from her ears. "That scream, didn't you hear it?"

Martha and Sam exchanged confused glances. "No," she shook her head and raised an open palm to feel the girl's forehead for a fever. "Might have been some animals out in the woods, hon."

Sam was studying Cassie's face. He was fairly certain that she was faking it, and that this was payback for the rubber snake he'd left in the shower for her to find this morning, but something about the look on her face made him wonder.

"It's probably some big branches rubbing together in the wind. They make a creepy sound," he said.

Cassie suddenly realized she was still kneeling and covering her ears, and she blushed, standing up quickly. She forced a smile, "Yeah, probably."

They began walking up the driveway again, and she stood back as her cousin and aunt walked into the house. As they stepped inside, she took one last look at the guest room window.

No one was there. Cassie took a deep breath and walked through the front door, closing it behind her.

* * *

The hallway was a dark cavern as Cassie wandered downstairs shortly after two in the morning. Thirsty, she was making her way to the kitchen, keeping one hand on the walls of the corridor as a guide. She reached the staircase and held on to the banister as she walked down. Grabbing a plastic tumbler out of the cabinets, she filled it with water from the kitchen sink and drank it in three large gulps. Cassie tossed the cup in the sink and turned around to go back upstairs.

She stopped when she reached the bottom of the staircase. The floorboards of the upstairs hallway were creaking. The figure she had seen in the window earlier that day entered her mind, and a chill washed over her body. Cassie took a shaky breath and whispered, "Sam? Is that you?"

The creaking sound stopped. She strained her eyes, struggling to make out any shapes in the darkness, then took one tentative step onto the staircase and ascended them carefully. By the time she reached the top, her hands were trembling. She stood there for a moment, frozen, still trying to make out any shapes in the dark. Though she could see nothing, Cassie could not shake the feeling that someone was watching her from the shadows.

Her bedroom door was on the left at the very end of the hall. All that stood between her and the relative safety of her bed were a few long strides. She steadied herself, inhaled sharply, and rushed down the hallway towards her room as if someone, or something, was at her heels.

Once inside, Cassie shut the door and flipped on the light. Immediately, she gasped at someone on the other side of the room. She laughed, realizing she had caught her own terrified reflection in the mirror. Shaking her head, she flipped the light back off and dove under the comforter.

Turning to lie on her left side, Cassie looked out the window which led out to the yard. Moonlight danced on the surface of the pumpkins, exaggerating their roundness. A small, sparkling layer of white frost covered the ground. Something about it was beautiful, yet menacing. She pursed her lips, took one last glance at the gleaming back acres, and flipped over to lie on her back.

Cassie's breath caught in her throat. The white figure from the window was floating above the foot of her bed. Now that it was closer, she could see that it was a woman. Her skin was almost as white as the gauzy material which seemed to float around her body rather than cover it. Her mouth was twisted in a scream of pain, and her eyes were circled with angry looking bruises. There was a giant, open wound in the center of her stomach. Thick strands of curly red hair twisted around her face, encircling her head like a crown.

Cassie screamed as the woman rushed her, her hands open and reaching for her throat.

* * *

Cassie woke up suddenly, shot up in bed, and ran to the mirror. She examined her neck closely, but found no marks. Then she ran to turn on the bedroom light, even though the sun was already shining brightly through the window. Shivering, she ran her hands over the comforter. The part at the foot of the bed was icy cold. She whipped around and flung the closet door open.

Nothing.

For a moment, she stood still, gathering the courage to bend down and look under the bed. Once again, there was nothing there. Cassie sat down and rubbed her face with both hands. She laid back down and tried to go to sleep, tossing restlessly until her aunt came knocking a few hours later.

"Coming down to breakfast?" Martha asked, not opening the door.

"Be right down!" Cassie answered, a little louder and a little more enthusiastically than she had intended.

* * *

"Sup, Rip?" Sam asked his cousin as he bit into a stack of pancakes.

Cassie rolled her eyes at him as she sat down at the table.

Martha smirked. "Be nice, Sam. It's 'Rip Van Winkle,' Cass. The old Washington Irving story about a man who falls asleep and when he wakes up—"

"—And when he finally wakes up, he's like two hundred years old," Sam interrupted, laughing.

"Have some pancakes," Martha smiled kindly at her niece, handing her an enormous stack on a bright red serving platter. "Bacon?" she asked.

She shook her head. "I'm good, thanks. Hey, I thought Washington Irving wrote 'The Headless Horseman.'"

"Actually, it's called 'The Legend of Sleepy Hollow,'" Sam said with a mouth full of pancakes. He swallowed. "The Horseman is just a character in it. And he wrote that one, too."

Cassie shrugged and looked at her plate. An obscene number of pancakes sat slathered in butter and maple syrup. It seemed like the wrong time to mention that she went gluten-free ten months ago, so she dug in, starving. She filled her glass with a pitcher of orange juice and gulped it. When she put the glass down, Martha and Sam were staring at her.

"Well," Martha said finally. "You guys finish up, take care of the dishes, and I'll head out back to finish harvesting the rest of the pumpkins. Only one week left until Halloween and people will be out and about today picking them up." She stood up, ruffled Sam's hair, and said, "Be nice," before walking out the front door to the produce cart.

Sam watched as Cassie continued to devour the food on her plate. "I'm gonna grab a shower. You clean up, Rip," he said, standing up and pushing his chair in. "Don't fall asleep."

Cassie rolled her eyes and watched her cousin leave the room as she finished her pancakes.

* * *

By the time Cassie made her way out back to the field, Sam was already loading several large pumpkins into the wagon. A shovel lay on the ground next to him.

"Ready to work?" Sam called out with a wave.

No, Cassie thought, waving back. She forced a smile and called out, "Sure!"

She walked over to the gourds and began picking them off of the vine and putting them into her wheelbarrow. As she looked up from the basket, something caught her eye in the distance. Between the trees in the woods bordering the farm, she spotted a small building. She pushed some hair from her eyes and squinted at it. "Hey, Sam?"

"What is it?" he asked, picking up the handles of the wheelbarrow and pulling it upright.

"Do you know what that is out there?" She pointed, and Sam's eyes followed.

"Oh, it's just storage now. It was my dad's workshop," he said.

Cassie felt a pang of guilt. It had been a few years since her uncle's disappearance, and she hadn't meant to bring it up. Even for a bully like Sam, it was far too cruel. "Sorry, I didn't know," she said.

Sam nodded and hauled the wagon off without another word, while Cassie kept her eyes locked on the small building.

* * *

Cassie woke that night to the feeling of pressure behind her on the bed. She was lying on her side facing the wall, and it distinctly felt as if someone was sitting on the edge of the bed behind her. She could hear breathing and what sounded like weeping.

Slowly, she turned. No one was there. She reached out from under the comforter and placed her hand on the bed. Just like that morning, it was cool to the touch. Gasping, Cassie took her hand away. She sat up and looked out the window. Fog was rolling in over the pumpkin patch, and out in the woods, a light was on in the shed.

She bolted out of bed and ran to the window to get a better look, but all she could see was the white glow of something in the shed window. Cassie looked at the bedroom door to make sure it was closed before opening her own window and leaning out to get a better view. Chilly autumn air flew into her room, blowing the curtains around her as she craned her neck to see. An uncontrollable urge washed over her.

She had to see what was glowing in that window.

Cassie slipped into a pair of jeans, put on some boots, and carefully stepped out of the window onto the trellis that hung on the side of the house, where she climbed down the ten feet onto the half-frozen grass. She took a deep breath before setting off toward the shed behind the field.

The leaves crunched under her feet as she walked, and she wrapped her arms around herself, wishing she had put on a jacket. When she came to the edge of the pumpkin patch, she turned around to face the house once more before stepping into the woods. Seeing that all the lights were off, she turned around to face the shed.

The small building was only a short distance away, yet somehow it loomed large over her. A white light was still glowing in the window, calling to her like the beacon of a lighthouse. Cassie took the final few steps toward the shed and paused. For a moment, she just stood in front of the door. She took a moment to gather her strength, then opened the door and stepped inside. As she did, a bolt of pain shot down from the top of her head, and she fell unconscious, to the ground.

* * *

Cassie was still in the shed, but it was no longer decrepit and worn. It was a beautiful workshop. A huge power-saw was set up on a large table, and wind chimes hung from the ceiling. The walls were lined with tools and hardware, and it smelled of freshly cut timber and her uncle's pipe tobacco. As Cassie took in the sight, the noise of the door opening startled her. A couple stumbled in: a handsome man of around forty and a younger woman with red hair that tumbled around her shoulders in great big curls.

"Jacob!" she yelled, "Uncle Jacob!" from her position on the floor. But he didn't turn.

He can't hear me. Am I dead?

Her uncle led the woman to the corner of the shed where there was a small love seat sofa, and they sat down next to each other. When the woman's face finally turned towards her, Cassie gasped.

She didn't recognize her. The pair kissed, and Cassie's face twisted in confusion. A sound startled her out of the daze, and she twisted to see who had burst through the now open front door.

Martha stood there, a wild, enraged look in her eyes. She was holding a double-barreled shotgun. Pumping the weapon, she pointed it at Jacob.

"No!" Cassie screamed as Martha fired the weapon and Jacob clutched at the wound now in his chest. His face wore a look of horror for just a few moments, until the expression faded away into nothing. Her uncle was dead. The woman next to him screamed and put her hands up as if to defend herself, but it was no use. Martha pumped the gun once more and shot her through the abdomen. The woman grabbed her stomach and held the wound, blood seeping from her hands. She moaned painfully as the life spilled out of her.

Cassie clutched her own stomach and screamed in agony. She could feel it, the hot, searing pain that was like an explosion in her guts. She could feel the woman's pain. After a few moments of painful gasping, the red-haired woman slumped over. The love seat was covered in blood, and some had pooled onto the floor. Both of the lovers were dead.

Martha's face was blank as she dropped the shotgun to the floor and walked over to the dead couple. One at a time, she dragged them out to the garden.

As quickly as it had come, the pain disappeared from Cassie's abdomen. She looked at Martha and screamed, "You bitch! What have you done?!"

Martha acted as if she could not hear her. Cassie stood up and tried to shove her aunt, but her hands fell through as if she was made of mist, and Cassie fell to the ground, crying. Martha dragged Jacob out first, and his dead-eyed stare seemed to follow Cassie as she got up and followed her aunt out into the garden.

She watched helplessly as Martha dug one deep grave and dumped both of the bodies in unceremoniously. Her face still wore a blank look as she walked back towards the shed, the shovel scraping across the ground as she pulled it behind her.

Cassie was in a state of horrified awe. It was as if a movie had just played out in front of her eyes, one that she wished she could un-see. She had watched her aunt brutally murder, then bury her uncle and a mystery woman in the backyard, in the same part of the farm where Cassie had spent the summer planting, and now the first weeks of fall gathering, the harvest.

The pumpkin patch.

* * *

"Cassie?" a gentle voice said. A hand was shaking her shoulder.

She opened her eyes and saw her aunt Martha looking down at her with concern. Instinctively, she jumped.

"Well, what's wrong, honey?" Martha asked. "What are you doing out here?"

Cassie struggled for words, her mouth open. "I... I must have been sleepwalking again," she lied, suddenly terrified of the woman in front of her.

Martha's expression changed slightly, her eyes narrowing to focus on Cassie. She broke into a smile. "Come on inside. It looks like you got a nasty bump there," she said, pointing at a spot on Cassie's head.

She reached up to touch and winced. Cassie couldn't remember anything falling on her. The last thing she recalled was walking into the shed, and then the pain came from the top of her head, and then... she had seen it. The horrible vision.

Uncle Jacob.

She had to suppress tears as Martha reached to help her up from the floor, and the two walked together back to the house. At the door, Cassie turned her head to look at the inside of the shed. A dark stain marred the floor in front of where the love seat had been in her vision. When they finally reached the house, Cassie turned once more to look through the field at the shed, where the white light was no longer glowing through the broken window.

* * *

Martha locked the door and turned on the wiper blades as Cassie sat down in the passenger seat of her van. The night after the incident in the shed, Cassie had called her parents and asked to come home. She was not supposed to fly out for another two weeks, but she had lied and told them she wanted to get a head start on her schoolwork for the year. Pleased at her apparent change in attitude, they had happily bought her a plane ticket. First class, even.

"Buckle up," Martha said, putting the car in gear and backing carefully out of the long, winding driveway.

The rain picked up as they rode silently down the winding country roads which led to the interstate. Cassie fidgeted in her seat as the windshield wipers swung like a metronome, keeping time with the storm outside. They rode for some time before Martha flipped the right turn signal on and merged, getting ready to exit the highway.

"Did you have a pleasant visit?" she said, finally breaking the silence.

Cassie practically jumped. "Y-yes. It was great. Thank you again for having me."

Martha smiled softly as they exited the highway for the freeway that would take them to the airport. "Good. I'm glad. Always nice for Sam to have company."

Cassie nodded and forced a smile back, silently thankful that they were now only a short distance from the terminal. They continued in silence for those last few miles, and Martha pulled the car up to the drop-off area of the small airport. She put the car in park and turned to Cassie, lifting one arm to put on her shoulder. Martha studied her niece's face for a moment before speaking. "Cassie?" she asked in a serious voice.

"Yes?" Her heart was pounding now.

Martha suddenly smiled widely. "Need any help getting your bags out?"

"No, I'm good. Thanks for everything. I had a great time. Tell Sam I said bye, ok?" She unbuckled her seatbelt and was reaching for the door handle when Martha grabbed her shoulder and dug in with her nails. Cassie froze, then slowly turned around to look at her aunt, whose eerily wide smile had faded into a grim sneer.

"How's that bump on your head?" she said, now smiling insanely, digging her nails deeper into the cloth of Cassie's jacket and making her wince.

She stared at her aunt with huge, fearful eyes. Martha's face had a wild but determined look on it. Cassie was too afraid to speak, and she darted her eyes around to see if anyone at the drop off area was looking at them. She wanted to cry out for help, but something in Martha's eyes scared her into silence.

"I've always been fond of you. It would be a shame if no one ever heard from you again," she said, her eyes a blank nightmare in the dark car. "Do we understand each other?"

Cassie nodded, her jaw slightly agape.

Martha's face relaxed and her smile became more natural. "Sure you don't need some help with your bags?" she asked.

Her lips still parted, Cassie shook her head. "No, I—I got it. Thanks." Faster than she had ever done anything, Cassie grabbed her duffel bag from the back seat and scurried out of the car. Once outside, she waved, bewildered, at her aunt, who waved back breezily, as if nothing out of the ordinary had happened.

In the bright lights of the airport terminal, she watched her aunt pull the car away slightly before stopping in front of a group of people crossing the road to walk into the airport. Cassie turned to go inside and was watching a security officer help an older woman with her bags when she felt a pull to look back at her aunt's car.

Cassie blinked hard twice. Two misty shapes were sitting directly behind Martha in the backseat. She opened her mouth to say something as one shape whipped around.

It was the same red-haired woman she had seen in the shed, and the woman raised a finger to her lips. Cassie closed her mouth and nodded as the car drove off. She watched as the woman turned around to face Martha, hands raised to close around her throat.

At this, Cassie smiled slightly, turning on her heels to walk inside the airport.

Next summer, she thought, I'm definitely going to camp.

LOUP GAROU

The old woman clutched her purse tightly as she walked down the dirt path from the old cathedral towards her home. She had never seen a robbery in her seventy-nine years in the small bayou town of Bidart, Louisiana, but she had been alive long enough to know that there is a first time for everything.

The hot, thicker-than-blood summer air hung around her limply, like a wet overcoat. Ruth didn't break a sweat as she walked, turning her head to see the old man in an even older rocking chair, staring out across the road into the bayou. His house was similarly old and worn, with just a few chips of white paint to show for what had once covered the entire house. The roof had partially caved in on one side, and he had patched it with an old sheet of tin on the other. The porch stairs were rickety, and one beam was so loose that it was almost sideways. A few nails stuck out around it, as if to add another layer of warning to anyone who might dare come visit old Leon.

The man watched her from his front porch, whistling a tune under his breath. He was palming something small and round in his hand, turning it repeatedly like a stone tumbling in a low tide.

The woman stopped in front of his house. "You've been missed at Holy Mass, Mr. Hermantraut," she said.

The old man continued turning the small object in his hand and said, in a voice harsh with age and tobacco, "Ruth, I haven't missed it at all."

The woman smiled slightly. "Alright then, you have a blessed day."

He grunted and watched as she turned back down the dirt path.

Ruth continued her steady pace all the way to her own modest home. It wasn't much better than the old man's, except that she had it repainted, so the outside wasn't cracking as much. She stopped at the front stoop to pull a few weeds from between the cracks in the stones and then walked inside. A screen door crashed behind her into the door frame, the spot worn from countless openings and closings over the years of family gatherings and visits from grandchildren.

Setting her purse on the small table in the front room, she walked down the hall to the bedroom. In front of the mirror, she took off her good jewelry—the pearls that she always wore to church—and placed them in a velvet box on the vanity table. She looked at her reflection in the mirror, at her still-beautiful, dark skin which didn't much belie her age, and combed a few stray hairs into place.

Behind her in the mirror was the reflection of her home altar. It was a modest wooden shelf her husband had built her in their first years of marriage. A statue of the Blessed Virgin sat to the right of a standing crucifix, with a flaming Sacred Heart emblazoned on Christ's chest. A rosary with hand-carved beads hung daintily from Mary's outstretched hands. A few small, white candles were strewn over the shelf, along with a small, shallow dish filled with holy water. Ruth walked over to it, dipped her fingers into the blessed water and made the sign of the cross. Then, she said a prayer for Leon Hermantraut as she had every day for fifty years, made the sign of the cross once more, and went to the kitchen to put on a pot of coffee.

* * *

Night fell and Leon was still on his porch, running his thumb over the small object in his hand. Ruth had not gotten close enough to see earlier, but if she had, she might have noticed its long, round shape and pointed tip, or the way the sun glinted off of its pure silver surface. When the sun finally dipped down over the bayou horizon, Leon grumbled a few words to himself before standing up and going inside.

The door creaked shut behind him as he thought of Ruth's earlier statement. The last thing he needed was a nosy church lady to go praying over his plans and ruining everything. Leon was no longer a young man himself, but he figured he had one good fight left in him. If this was to be that fight, well, that would be just fine.

The old man walked into his tiny kitchen. It was a few degrees warmer, and definitely more humid, inside his house than out, but he simply wiped his brow as he opened a can of pork and beans to put on the stove for supper. While it warmed up, Leon walked into his bedroom. He placed the object he had been palming into a ceramic tray at his bedside table, and it landed with a clink against a single gold band which matched the one still on his left ring finger.

Leon went to wash up for dinner, splashing a bit of not-quite-clear water into his face, letting the sweat and dirt of the day come off of him. He looked at his reflection in the mirror. If Ruth's skin was café au lait, Leon's was espresso—dark and strong. Unlike Ruth, however, Leon's face was drawn long with time and sorrow.

The old man was a favorite of town gossip, and his only supporter against the rumors was his neighbor, Ruth. "It takes a bite out of you, grief," she often reminded people who remarked how Leon wasn't looking too good these days. "You end up like an old apple, all eaten up except for the core of you." And in that estimation she was right, for Leon looked every bit of his seventy-eight years.

He crossed himself before sitting down at his small kitchen table and said a short, simple prayer. "Thank you, I'm grateful. Forgive me, I'm sorry."

He finished dinner and walked back to his bedside table where he opened the drawer and retrieved a pistol, then picked up the small object from the ceramic tray and went out to the porch, where he sat quietly for several more hours. The beast he was waiting for didn't come as quickly as he had expected, and in the moonlit glow of night, the old man dozed on his porch. As he did, a series of images flashed before his eyes, the same ones he had seen every night for fifty years.

Visions of the night his family was taken from him.

Horrible, sharp screams had come from the children's bedroom. His wife jumped out of bed, throwing the blanket off of herself as she did. Leon woke up to see her nightgown billowing behind her as she ran out of their darkened room, and he shot up to follow her into their children's bedroom.

Then another scream, an unfamiliar sound. It was a scream of grief from his wife, who was on her knees at the window in their children's room. The children were nowhere to be found. The beds were empty—the blankets clawed to shreds. The window to their room, which faced the swamp to the back, was open, and the flimsy curtains flailed in the hot summer wind. She continued to scream, and as Leon looked in disbelief at the scene, her screams faded as if she was suddenly very far away. He could not make sense of what he was seeing. His wife's nightgown blowing behind her as she climbed out of the tiny window shook him out of the momentary shock.

"Tessa, wait!" Leon screamed as he tried to grab for his wife, but it was too late. She was out the window and running through the backyard to the swamp. He rushed to the windowsill and climbed, but stopped when he felt something sharp on the palms of his hands. He lifted them from the window frame and froze—deep, coarse claw marks were etched into the wood, like a wild beast had broken in. Again, he froze until a new scream shook him. Ignoring the pain, he crawled out of the window and ran out into the yard.

"Tessa!"

By the time he heard the final round of screams from his wife, it was too late. Leon got to the edge of their yard where the swamp began just in time to watch his wife being dragged into the murky water by her waist.

"Help me, oh God!" she screamed, clawing at the Spanish moss hanging overhead, as if she could climb it to safety.

It was then, in the pale moonlight, that Leon finally laid eyes upon the beast that carried her.

The thing stood upright like a human, but was as big as a bear. Great, coarse tufts of fur covered it, and it bared its teeth in a sneer that would put the most rabid of dogs to shame. The claws were its most frightening attribute. Long and talon-like, even from a distance, Leon could see that they were digging into the flesh of his wife's waist, pinning her and pulling her back. He stepped into the dark swamp water and tried to run towards her, stepping blindly into the muck and grime, but it was too late. His wife and the beast had disappeared into the rows of Cyprus trees that grew like weeds in the swamp as he heard her last screams.

"Leon, help me, please!" she cried, her voice echoing through the moss which seemed to sway with the force of her final breaths. The moon shone down through the trees as the last thing Leon saw of his wife was a flicker of light glinting off of her modest gold wedding band while she waved her arms, crying out for help.

The image of the moon shining off of his wife's ring haunted him. As Leon loaded the shotgun in his lap, he thought of the aftermath of that night. Search parties had crawled the swamp and bayou for weeks. A police report had been filed, of course, and his dutiful neighbor Ruth had ensured that a mass was said for the Hermantraut family.

But Leon could see it in people's eyes as they went through the motions of searching and praying for his family: they would never find his family. The townsfolk knew as well as he did. The beast, the Loup Garou, had taken them.

For years, people had tried to convince him that a giant gator had been responsible. But he could still see in some of their eyes, the old-timers especially, that they knew the real culprit. They had grown up hearing the same stories Leon had, and they knew.

The Loup Garou was alive—was *hungry*—and every fifty years, needed to sate that terrible hunger.

Ruth could keep her church and her candles and her prayers. Leon had a single silver bullet, and that would be enough.

WRAITH OF WEST END WOODS

It felt like they had been in the car for years when the Downing family van finished its fifteen hundred mile trip from Oconomowac, Wisconsin to West End, Maine. It was early August, hot, and the air conditioning in the van was broken, so sticky, warm air flowed in the open windows. The circulating air helped a bit, but it didn't cool it down much. Mr. Downing navigated the sleepy hills and turns of the thick pine forest and, at the bottom of one hill, a small cemetery stood slanted as if it bore its back against the passing of time. Just past its wrought-iron gates, a sign peeked up over the grass.

"HERE 'TIS"

"Why is it spelled that way?" Sally Downing asked. She was rubbing the sleep out of her eyes and sitting up in a pile of blankets in the middle seat of the van.

Mrs. Downing stretched her arms out in the passenger seat and smiled, yawning. "Well, it's just how people talk out here. It just means we're there now. As in: 'Here it is, we've arrived.'"

"Finally," a voice came from the back seat. Mick Downing took his headphones off and craned his neck to look out the window to his left. "Who builds a house next to a cemetery?" he muttered.

"Mick..." Mr. Downing said in an admonishing tone, waving as he pulled into the driveway of a blue clapboard house. A gray-haired, petite woman stood next to a tall white-haired man who waved back with only three and a half fingers—a wood-working accident. "Your mom's family is a little spooky, is all," Mr. Downing said under his breath as he drove down the hill into the driveway.

"Ted," Carol Downing said, pinching his arm playfully as he put the car in park. She unbuckled her seat belt and stepped out of the car, stretching before she walked over and hugged her aunt and uncle. The kids unbuckled their seat belts and made their way out of the car as their father walked around the front of it towards the old woman.

"Hey there, kids!" the old man laughed.

"You made it," the old lady smiled, her voice smaller than her husband's.

"Good to see you all," Mr. Downing said, and the old lady smiled as he bent down to hug her.

Ted reached over and shook the old man's hand. "Rob, thanks for having us again."

"Of course!" he shook his hand back and grinned widely, exposing large, straight teeth. Rob had high cheekbones and, at nearly seven feet tall, towered over his petite wife. She was smiling too, hunched over and frail. "Bessie," the old man said, "Shall we let them get settled and get suppah ready?"

She nodded and reached a hand out to Carol, who helped the frail old woman up the front stoop and into her house. Rob watched them walk in, then gestured for the rest of the family to follow. "All aboard!" he yelled. Faded naval tattoos stuck out from the sleeves of the old man's shirt, a grey-green reminder of the past.

* * *

"Wow, this looks great!" Carol said as the six of them settled in at the table, her hair still wet from the shower. She brushed some strands from her face and sat down.

"Oh, thank you," Bessie said with a smile as her husband of fifty-five years helped her sit down. "It's just lasagna. I get the recipe off the box," she said with one hand raised to the side of her mouth, as if revealing a torrid secret.

"Put your napkin in your lap, Sally," Ted said, pointing at the gingham napkins, carefully folded at each place setting.

Mick took the serving platter from the middle of the table and plopped an enormous piece of lasagna onto his plate before passing it on to Rob. He took a large bite and said, "It's good," with a mouth full of food.

"Manners, Mick," Carol said as she reached for a knot of garlic bread on the table.

"That's enough," Sally said with wide eyes as her father put a large serving on her plate. The mountain of food looked huge in front of her tiny frame.

Bessie turned to the girl and said, "Now dear, you don't need to eat all of that. And if you don't like it, I will pour you some cereal."

"No, she'll eat it. Just take a bite, sweetie," Carol said, nodding with raised eyebrows at Sally, who nodded back, looking between her mom and Bessie.

"This is great, thank you, Bess," Ted said. He was almost halfway finished with his plate and marinara sauce trailed down his shirt.

Seeing that, Rob let out a deep laugh that echoed throughout the wooden house. Settling down, he asked, "So, what do you folks have planned for tomorrow?"

Carol and Ted looked at each other. "I'm not sure exactly," she said. "Maybe go to the beach?"

"Yeah!" Sally cried. There was a single, tiny fork-full of lasagna missing from her plate.

"Ayuh, that's an idea," Rob said. "We have plenty of books if you want some beach reading." He gestured towards the open door that led down into the basement, where the Downing family was sleeping for the week. They lined the stairs with shelves upon shelves of books. A few were new, but most had faded. The stairway had the pleasant, musty odor of an old library.

"I saw that," Mick said. "Where did you get all of those?"

Rob smiled. "Oh, here and there. Help yourself, take a few home with you if you like."

"Thanks," Mick said, still chewing. His mom shot him a look, and he closed his mouth.

* * *

Mick turned off the hot water and reached for a towel. The others had gone to bed, and he had taken a shower. Since he was sharing a room with his family for the week, he figured this was his shot at privacy and took his time, enjoying the hot steam filling the room.

Stepping out onto the cold tile floor, he stood in front of the mirror, wiping the fog off of it with one hand. He lifted the towel to his face and inspected it in the mirror, his cheeks flushed from the heat. Taking a deep breath, he dried off, got dressed, and walked out to the main area of the basement.

His mother was asleep, with Sally nestled up against her, snoring. His dad was also snoring, sitting on the large recliner. A remote rested in his hands, threatening to fall out and onto the floor at any minute. Mick tip-toed over and slipped the remote out of his father's hand and turned off the tv. As the screen flashed to black, he gasped, frozen.

A figure had appeared in the reflection on the screen.

Mick jumped around to look out the doors that lead out of the basement and into the woods in the back, but only the light of the moon filled the yard. He shook his head and climbed into the sofa bed, still looking out the patio doors, pulling the blanket up to just under his wide eyes.

Moonlight glinted off of the boughs of the ancient pine trees that filled the woods behind the house. Shadows danced between them and cicadas buzzed loudly. He surveyed the scene, straining his eyes against the dark. Mick couldn't make out anything, but he had the distinct feeling that someone was staring back at him from the woods.

Probably an animal.

He turned around and forced his eyes shut. Mercifully, sleep came quickly.

* * *

Mick woke up to the sound of rain pummeling the doors which lead out of the basement and out to the backyard. He sat up and rubbed his eyes. His family was nowhere to be seen. The sound of coughing was coming from the bathroom, followed by his parents' voices.

Groggy, he got up and walked towards the sound. He stood in the doorway, and saw his parents comforting his little sister, who was taking a bath. She was pale and looked rather pitiful. "What's up?" he asked, yawning.

His mom was crouched in front of Sally, holding a cool rag to her forehead, and his father was searching through the medicine cabinet next to the sink. "She's been up sick all night," she said.

"No beach then today, huh?" Mick asked.

Both his parents shot him a scolding look.

"Sorry," he grinned sheepishly. "Hey, kid," Mick said to Sally, who turned to look at him with big brown eyes, "It's raining today anyhow. We'll get to the ocean tomorrow, maybe." Sally's pout turned into a kind of smile, and Mick smiled back.

He washed his face and brush his teeth despite all four of them crammed in the tiny bathroom and then walked back out to the basement. Standing in front of the doors, he looked out into the woods. He smiled, thinking how foolish he had been last night. *These woods are harmless*, he thought. *Nothing but pine trees and squirrels*. The rain was dying down, and he thought he spotted a trail out in the distance that led through the thick rows of trees.

Mick bounded upstairs and walked to the kitchen cabinets to get a bowl and some cereal.

"Morning!" a voice bellowed behind him.

He spun around and saw Bessie and Rob sitting in their chairs in the living room. His uncle was whittling a small chunk of wood and his aunt was crocheting something large and blue.

"Mickey, would you like me to fix you something to eat?" she asked.

"No, no, don't get up. Cereal is good," Mick smiled, walking his bowl to the table.

Rob stopped his whittling and stared at Mick with dark eyes. "Guess your sisters come down with something?"

Through a mouthful of rice cereal, Mick said, "Yeah, I guess."

The old couple shared a knowing, concerned look before Rob went back to his whittling and Bessie took up her knitting needles again.

"Well, what have you got planned for today?" she asked.

Still chewing, Mick shrugged. "I dunno. Might go on a run through the woods back there. It looks like there's a trail I could follow. I'm missing cross country camp coming out here, so it will be good for me to get in a long run."

Rob stopped his whittling and Bessie's crocheting needles fell out of her hands. They looked at each other, then back at Mick.

"It's supposed to rain all day," Rob said.

"Nah, it looks like it's clearing up," Mick said, not looking up from his cereal.

"Mick," Bessie said gently, "Maybe you'd better stay in and help your folks with Sally. I'm sure they'd appreciate the extra pair of hands."

He looked up finally and saw they were both staring at him. Their eyes wore a look that was unfamiliar to Mick—a mix of fear and admonishment. Startled a bit by the foreignness of their gaze, he said, "I won't be gone long."

Bessie, turning her gaze from Mick, now looked at Rob with pursed lips.

"Be careful out there, now," Rob said, his eyes narrowed. "Folks have gotten lost out there, and the trail is awfully narrow in some parts."

Mick finished his cereal and nodded, walking his bowl to the sink. "Sure thing. Hey, can you tell my parents where I went if they ask? They're still down in the bathroom with Sally."

"Now, Mick—" Rob started.

"I'll be fine," Mick interjected with a smile. "I've done plenty of back country running. I won't even be gone an hour."

"Well," Rob said, clearing his throat, "Keep your eyes open."

Bessie nodded in agreement.

"Yeah, sure thing," Mick said, eyeing them closely before disappearing again down the basement stairs.

Rob and Bessie listened to his footsteps, and the old woman raised a hand to her mouth and looked out the window. Rob reached out to pat her on the arm.

* * *

As Mick walked down the stairs, he thought about the old folks' apprehension. He only saw them every few years, so part of him was unsurprised that they treated him as if he was a small child. Still, something in their eyes had unsettled him. They weren't senile—his father's parents had both suffered from dementia, and he knew what that looked like.

What are they so afraid of?

A chill ran over him, and he shrugged it off, deciding instead to prepare for his run. Mick put on a pair of track shorts and a maroon sleeveless shirt that said *"Milton High Commodores Cross Country."* He dug through his backpack for earbuds and tennis shoes. Humming, he laced the shoes up and plugged the earbuds into his phone before opening the patio doors that led out into the backyard.

The yard comprised a small clearing, surrounded by rows of pine trees, and their fallen needles covered the ground like a thick blanket. Mick stretched his arms and looked around, taking deep breaths of the fresh air. It smelled of pine and of the ocean, which was only thirty miles west of his aunt and uncle's home. After a few more stretches, Mick took off into West End Woods.

Only a few minutes passed by before he was short of breath. He had spent the first half mile running up a steep hill and was now at the top. Mick slowed as he reached it and bent over with his hands on his knees.

This is no good, he thought. *Taking the summer off from running might have been a bad idea.*

Practice was starting in two weeks, and he could barely run a mile without getting winded. Shaking his head, he took another big breath and set off again down the hill.

The trail at the bottom of the hill turned sharply into a grove of pine trees that were packed together tightly. They were wide and incredibly tall, some of them obviously hundreds of years old. Mick was looking up at them when suddenly he felt a branch snag on his shirt. He stopped to untangle himself, humming along to a Ramones song on his iPhone.

He looked down at his shirt and began to untangle himself from the branch when the hairs on the back of his neck pricked up. Goosebumps covered his skin, and he was suddenly afraid to look up. But, slowly, he did.

A woman in a grey sack-cloth dress stood several feet in front of him on the narrow trail. Her arms were unnaturally straight at her sides, and black and gray hair flowed from her head in long strings that looked like yarn. She was heaving in great breaths, each one audible above the wind—a combination of screaming and breathing. Her face, though, is what made Mick gasp.

She had bright green eyes which bore the look of insanity, and the bottom half of her face was missing—in its place, a fleshless lower mandible. She opened her mouth, and a gush of blood spilled out and onto the ground. One long string of blood dripped slowly from what was left of her face as her panting grew louder and quicker.

Mick dropped his phone and stumbled backwards, his face contorted in fear and confusion. The woman took a step towards him and he regained his composure just long enough to grab his phone off of the ground, get up, and start running.

As he sprinted back down the path, he could hear her behind him. Adrenaline coursed through his veins and his legs pumped. The woman's breathing grew increasingly louder until she was shrieking with every breath as she chased him out of the woods.

Mick felt her clawing at the back of his shirt, and he screamed. He was approaching the top of the hill now, and if he could just make it back down to the bottom, that would lead him into his aunt and uncle's backyard and he could get inside the house through the basement doors. He would be safe.

Mick could still feel hot breath on his neck, and the flesh on his back burned where she had clawed him, as if it had been cut by white hot razors. With a last burst of adrenaline, he reached the top of the hill. Not daring to turn around to look at what was chasing him, he sprinted back down towards the house, realizing for the first time that the screams he was hearing were his own. Mick entered the clearing and took one look back at the woods before throwing himself at the patio doors.

The woman was standing at the top of the hill. She was still taking large, heaving, screeching breaths, and her arms were still unnaturally resting at her sides.

He burst through the patio doors, crying.

"Mick, what's wrong!" his mom asked, running out from the basement bathroom.

He looked up at her through tears and she ran to him and brushed the hair, sweat, and tears from his face.

His dad burst out of the bathroom behind her. "What happened?" He saw Mick's face and ran towards him. "Where were you?"

Mick collapsed on the ground, panting. Between breaths, he said, "I went for a run, out in the woods." He was choking back tears, "There was a woman, she was all bloody, and she chased me!"

His parents exchanged a worried glance before helping him up and onto the couch. As they did, footsteps came from the stairway.

"Everything ok down there?" Rob bellowed as he walked. When he got down to the basement and saw Mick, he paused.

Mick's eyes brightened when he saw him. "What's out there? What the hell is out there?!" he cried.

"Mick!" his father said.

Rob waved a hand. "It's alright," he said, "Why don't you check on Sally? I'll sit here with the boy for a spell."

Mick's parents looked at each other and nodded reluctantly. His mom brushed the hair out of his head and kissed him on the forehead before walking to the back room where Sally lay asleep.

Rob sat down on the couch next to Mick and slapped his hands on his knees. He stared ahead for a few minutes before turning his head to look at the boy. "Now, son," he said, his face stern, "I know what you saw. And I'm going to tell you what it was, but they will not believe you, so don't bother," he said, pointing towards the back room where his parents were. "What you saw was the Wraith."

"Wraith?" Mick whispered.

The old man nodded. "When this town, West End, was first settled, yellow fever was going around. Killed many people, especially young children. There was an old woman who lived alone in the woods, not far from where this house stands. Because she was old and lived alone, rumors went around that she was a witch, and that she had cursed the town for shunning her."

Mick stared at Rob as he talked, his eyes wide with fear.

"At first, that's all there was to it—rumors. But after more children succumbed to the fever, those rumors grew until the townsfolk actually believed that they were true. You'll find, as you get older, that when people need something to blame, they'll find it. So," Rob continued, wiping his face with his hands, "A few of the town elders gathered and stormed her house in the middle of the night. They dragged her out and tortured her, trying to get her to confess to cursing them. Well, she never did, of course. So, they hanged her. As a witch."

Mick's mouth opened slightly as he struggled for words.

Rob continued, "Problem was, after she died, the deaths didn't stop. In fact, things got worse. People who went into the woods disappeared, and more children died of the fever. Only a few families stayed in West End. Ours being one of them."

"Is it safe here? I mean, how do you live here with it so close?"

Rob stared at him. "I have respect for the woods, and for the Wraith. We don't step foot into her territory. You go out there, and you're walking onto her turf. If the rumors are true, and she cursed the children... well, in death, she could be even stronger."

Mick's eyes widened.

"The fairy tale is true. The curse is real, that's what I'm trying to say. Now, your sister is sick, and why do you think that is?" Rob said.

"Everything ok out here?" Mick's dad said, walking out from the back room.

"Yeah, dad, it's fine," Mick answered, still looking at Rob.

His dad ducked back into the back room at the sound of Sally having another coughing fit.

"So what do I do?" Mick whispered.

"Don't go back into the woods. Leave her to rest in peace," Rob said, standing up.

"Why did you let us come here if you knew this could happen?" Mick asked.

"I've lived here my whole life," Rob said, standing at the foot of the stairs. "I've never lost a child, and I wanted the rumors to be just that. Rumors. But after what you saw, and with your sister... well, I'd rather not take a chance. Would you?"

Mick shook his head, and Rob nodded in response. As the old man lumbered up the stairs, Mick got up from the couch and walked to the patio doors.

Across the yard, at the top of the hill, the woman was standing, staring. He had to strain his eyes to see, but Mick could swear that through her broken jaw, the Wraith was grinning.

BLACK-EYED CHILDREN

Eric looked at the clock from his position on the couch.

It was 11:30 p.m.

The owner of the house wouldn't be home for at least another three hours. He leaned back with one hand behind his head and grabbed the remote, enjoying the feeling of the overhead fan blowing cool air through his long hair.

That was the problem with Chicago, in his estimation: you spend all winter thinking the snow and freezing wind will never stop, and when summer finally rolls around, the black pavement seems to radiate the heat so much that you're almost—*almost*— wishing for snow again. Now deep into the dog days of summer, Eric was ready for winter. Cooler weather meant the people he house-sat for would take more trips out to their home in Hawaii, and more money earned for just sitting around.

Eric reached for the coffee table, took a huge swig out of his soda, and grabbed another handful of chips, crunching loudly as he channel-surfed. He flipped to the nightly news, where a woman was teetering on ridiculous heels while reporting the weather.

A knock came at the door, and Eric jumped. He peered around the foyer from his position on the couch to get a look at who was at the door without sitting up. The front door was glass but overlaid with a checkered pattern so that the view was muddled. He let out an annoyed sigh and turned the tv on mute before getting up to check the door.

The floorboards creaked beneath his feet as he walked, reminding him of the home's age. It was a historic downtown neighborhood, and none of the homes were worth less than two million dollars. Rich owners meant big paydays. When he got to the door, he reached for the handle and then quickly drew his hand back, stopped by an inexplicable urge to check the peephole before opening it.

No one was there. All he could see were the front steps illuminated by automatic flood lights. He jerked the door open and called out, "Hello?"

A few moments after the words left his lips, two little figures stepped out from behind a porch beam. He breathed a small sigh of relief.

Kids. Just kids.

The older one was a girl, perhaps nine, with short, white hair that stuck out in several directions, and she held the hand of a small boy of around five with dark, curly hair.

"What are you two doing out so late?"

The kids kept their faces down, looking at the cement steps for a few moments before the girl spoke up in a frightened little voice. "We need to call our mother. May we use your phone?"

Eric kept his hand on the door and looked around the porch to see if anyone was watching. The kids didn't look like they were from anywhere near this neighborhood. Their clothes were ragged, and the little boy was missing a shoe.

"Um," he stalled, "Where is your mother? How did you guys get here?" Eric turned his head to look around the street for people they could have come with.

"We need to use your phone. Please," the girl said again. This time, however, her voice had a different, almost demanding tone.

Eric bristled at the change in her voice and shut the door a little, shrinking the space between the door and the frame so that only his head was poking out. It was hard to see much under the porch light, and he squinted to get a better look at their faces. Then, both children looked up for the first time.

Their eyes were solid black, like dark marbles set in their skulls.

Eric inhaled sharply at the sight. It was horrifying and somehow grotesque, and his stomach churned as he fought to remove his eyes from their gaze. For a moment, it felt like they locked him into them, and he'd never be able to look away.

Mercifully, a cat meowed in the alley and a trash can fell over, and the sound startled him out of his trance. He shook his head and said, "I'm sorry, I can't help you," as he fumbled to shut the door, turning all four locks back into place.

"You have to let us in!" the girl shouted from the other side of the door. The sound made him jump, and he took several steps back into the foyer.

The kids pounded on the door with their fists, their voices now deeper and more menacing.

"We need to call our mother!"

"Let us in!"

Eric reached to turn off the light in the living room, darkening the house, and sat back down on the couch. He pulled a blanket over himself and turned up the volume on the television. The pounding continued for a few moments, but they never made another sound. He turned on old cartoons and, after a few very tense hours, fell asleep on the couch.

* * *

When Eric woke up, the television was still on, but an infomercial had replaced the cartoons. A middle-aged man with a white ponytail was in the middle of demonstrating how to use the latest non-stick ceramic pan, when he paused and looked at the cameras.

"Let us in, Eric."

The breath caught in Eric's throat as he sat up. The man with the white ponytail locked eyes with him.

"I said: Let us in, Eric."

Without understanding why he was doing it, Eric nodded his head. He found he could not turn his gaze away from the man on the screen. Suddenly, the sound of cars honking outside startled him out of his trance. He sat up and screamed.

"No!"

On the tv screen, the man's face changed, morphing into something angular and demonic with glowing, red eyes. He spoke again, his voice a deep, angry roar.

"You will let us in!"

Eric screamed as the face rushed towards him through the television screen. As if his body was trying to protect him, he passed out in a heap on the couch.

* * *

A hand shook his shoulder to wake him, and Eric bolted upright and looked around. He was still in the stately old home. He looked at the hand shaking his shoulder and followed it up to the person trying to wake him.

"Eric, I'm home. Are you alright?"

An older woman dressed casually in expensive leisure wear stood in front of him, looking every bit her age. It was Grace, the owner of the house. Her hair and makeup were styled as elegantly as ever, but her face wore a look of concern he had never seen before. There was something else in her eyes that was unfamiliar. With horror, he realized it was fear. Yes, she was afraid, and her faded blue eyes were searching his face for answers.

He rubbed his face. "Yes, I'm fine. I didn't hear you come in, sorry." Eric picked up his belongings. "How was the trip?" he asked as he bent over, shoving his books and sweatshirt into a bag, wanting to get out of the house and back to his dorm as quickly as possible. When Grace didn't answer right away, he looked up.

She sank into an antique wingback chair opposite of where he had been sleeping, hands clasped firmly in her lap, studying them. She moved her gaze to his and brought a hand to her mouth.

Eric tilted his head slightly. "Is everything alright?" As the words left his mouth, he heard the sirens. "Grace—"

"It's the neighbors," she said. "The Yeardleys. All of them," she muttered, getting up from the chair to look out the front window.

Eric stood up and followed her. Across the street, medics were rolling gurneys out of a historic cobblestone house. Each one wore a full hazmat suit. Ten police cars lined the street, their lights on. A group of officers stood huddled off to the side, murmuring and smoking cigarettes. As they did, a black car pulled up. It looked like a government car, maybe federal. Eric shook his head in disbelief.

"What happened? Are they—"

"All of them," Grace repeated, her voice cracking. "The officer told me. They barely let my driver pull up to the house." Suddenly, she turned to look at the young man who had been watching her house every summer for the past four years. "Eric," she said, "did you see anything strange last night? Anything at all?"

He paused for a moment before answering.

"No."

She studied his face as the memory of the previous night flashed in his mind—the horrible children with their black eyes, the way they had somehow captured him in a trance. And then, the thing on the television screen. Surely that had been a dream. A terrible coincidence.

He stood up to leave, and Grace handed him the usual envelope of cash with a shaky hand. He reached to take it and she held his hand there for a second, looking up at him.

"Be careful, Eric," she whispered.

Nodding, he grabbed the rest of his belongings and practically sprinted out the front door and down the steps to the street. He kept his eyes on his feet as he walked, refusing to look at any of the medics, and especially avoided looking at any of the gurneys.

Eric quickened his pace to a slow jog and headed towards the train stop. Just a quick ride on the red line of the L stood between him and never seeing that house, or that neighborhood, ever again. He wasn't sure how to break the news to Grace. She had always been so kind to him, but he knew he could never go back. Whatever got to the Yeardleys—

"All of them."

— that night had tried to get to him first.

He swiped his student pass and walked through the turn-styles just as the train car pulled to a stop. Eric looked around first to see if anyone else would hop on with him and found no one. Relieved, he stepped on board.

He settled into a seat and put on his headphones, scrolling through his phone to find some music to take his mind off of the previous night. The doors slid closed and the whirring sound of the train's engine revved in his ears, audible even over his music.

Putting his phone back in his coat pocket, he paused. A few hairs had stood up on the back of his neck. Eric turned his head.

At the back of the train compartment sat a familiar-looking pair of children. Both their eyes were completely black. As he opened his mouth to scream, they opened theirs as well, revealing rows of horrible, pointed teeth.

* * *

The train conductor turned his head as they entered the tunnel. Above the noise of the train's engine and the whir of the wheels on the track, he thought he heard a strange sound. He strained his ears to listen for a moment, and it continued.

They were just a few moments from the next stop, and he got up to look out the back compartment of the engine room at the passenger car.

Two kids, a boy and a girl, sat on either side of a young man riding the train. The young man was slumped over. It wasn't unusual. People often slept on the train. He half-smiled in relief.

The smile faded from the conductor's face as both of the children snapped their heads to look at him, revealing two sets of black, shark-like eyes.

WENDIGO

Kate navigated her car through the sharp, foggy bends of Highway 89 deep in the mountains of the Sierra Nevadas. As she drove, the words echoed in her ears.

"Check, please!"

It was how her date had responded to her not thirty minutes earlier.

"So, are you looking for a relationship right now, trying to settle down?" he grinned through a professionally whitened set of porcelain veneers.

Kate blushed. She *was* interested in settling down, preferably as soon as possible; but, then again, *"Nice girls don't act desperate."* That was something her mother used to say. Well, either her mother had said it, or one of the nuns at her grade school. Kate often confused the two. So, she had smiled politely and glanced at the bottle of red wine on the table, their two full glasses, and the order of calamari which had just arrived.

"Oh, I'm not sure, but I am enjoying some very good company right now," Kate answered diplomatically. The polite, coy smile remained on her face, and candlelight glinted off of her brown eyes.

He smiled back for a moment, and then his face darkened. "In that case, this date is over. I'm tired of buying steak dinners for women without getting anything in return."

Kate's jaw dropped as her date leaned in closer and gestured toward the food and drinks on their table. "By the way, we're splitting the bill." He leaned back, put a hand in the air, and called out for the server. "Check, please!"

Kate shook her head as she drove, the words replaying themselves in her head. "No more online dating," she swore to herself through pursed lips.

As her car wound through the misty roads, her mind wandered to what her next move should be. *Maybe meet a man at a bar the old-fashioned way?* She winced at the thought.

The road was steep and lined with thick rows of pine trees, and the fog thickened. She squinted, reaching to turn on the fog lights and windshield wipers. It wasn't raining, but the fog was so dense that condensation had formed on the windshield. Autumn in the Sierras was typically rainy and muggy, and today had been no exception. Now that it was nightfall, the darkness combined with the fog made it difficult to see more than thirty yards ahead.

Kate heard her phone beep in her purse and turned her head for just a second to reach inside. Typically, she made a point of turning off the device before she drove. Kate had little patience for people who used their phones while driving, but she had been so flustered and upset by the *"Check, please!"* guy that it had slipped her mind completely.

She looked at the light briefly and couldn't resist reading the message lit up in green on her phone. She wished for a split second it was her date apologizing for his behavior, and hated herself for the thought. *You're not* that *desperate.* She glanced down at the lit screen, turning her eyes away from the road for a brief second. It was from her roommate.

"How did it go?"

Suddenly, she felt the tires slip on the right side and realized she was swerving into the ditch.

"Shit!" Kate screamed, dropping her phone and gripping the wheel with both hands just in time to turn away from a steep drop-off to her right. She corrected the vehicle and, shaking, took a few deep breaths and closed her eyes. Upon opening them, she screamed.

A figure stood illuminated in front of her car. It was upright on its hind legs, which were bent backwards unnaturally at the knee, and wore some kind of cloak that was ragged and torn. The fabric barely covered its skin, which looked like that of a dog missing large patches of hair. Its arms were long and ended in claws, which it held out with open palms. The beast had the head of a goat with giant horns and cavernous sockets where eyes should have been. Its teeth were large and pointed like a coyote's.

Kate stopped screaming long enough to shift the car into reverse and turn the car around. The car spun, and the wheels kicked up rocks as she sped back in the direction she'd come from.

Tears burned her eyes, and she refused to look into the rearview mirror.

"I'm upset. It's foggy out and my eyes are playing tricks on me," she said aloud, her voice breaking as she spoke. Kate pressed her foot harder on the gas pedal and glanced quickly at the dashboard as she heard it ding. The gas tank was nearly empty. She remembered a little gas station at the foot of the mountain and breathed a tiny sigh of relief.

I'll stop there. Get a cold drink and fuel up, settle my nerves.

Kate navigated the roads with wide eyes as she drove back down the mountain. She was at once terrified of seeing the thing she saw earlier, and afraid of not seeing it. If it was sneaking around her unnoticed, somehow... well, somehow that would be worse.

After what seemed like hours, the lights of a Country Mart Station sign shone through her windshield. She flipped the turn signal on and slowed down, pursing her lips to exhale slowly. Kate pulled the car up to one of the gas tanks and looked at herself in the garish lights that shone through her car windows. Her mascara h smeared, and she wiped as much of it off as she could with the back of one hand and brushed the stray hairs from out of her face before getting out of the car.

There wasn't another soul in sight, and her heels clicked against the gravelly pavement as she trudged toward the attached convenience store. She turned her head from side to side, still wary, senses piqued and attuned to anything out of the ordinary.

A short jingle played as she pushed the glass doors open and stepped into the store. The smell of stale food, walk-in freezers, and beef jerky hit her nose and was surprisingly comforting after an evening of unfamiliarity. She turned to the cash register where a dark-haired man was leaning back in a chair, reading a motorcycle magazine.

"Hello," she squeaked out, trying to make her presence known. The last thing she needed was to be blown away by some nervous cashier with a shotgun.

The papers in the magazine rustled as the man, startled, sat up straighter and set it down on the counter. His eyes were dark but friendly, and long dark hair hung down low over his eyebrows. "Good evening, Señora," he nodded.

She nodded back primly and stood in the snack aisle of the mart, trying to stall. Kate did not want to go back out into the dark, into the wild unknown where that thing she saw could appear at any moment. Kate felt eyes on her and turned around. The cashier was looking her over, not lewdly, but with suspicion. She realized that she probably looked strange, alone in the mountains, dressed for a night out. She had also been staring at a bag of pretzels for the better part of five minutes as she pondered what her next move should be. Suddenly embarrassed, she smiled back at him and grabbed the pretzels. Kate walked to the cooler and grabbed a can of Coke, then made her way to the register. She cleared her throat as she set the items down.

The man sat up in his chair and she saw his name tag, which read *"Manny."*

He cleared his throat. "You alright?"

"Hmm? Oh, yes," she said, eking out a small smile.

Manny grabbed her items and ran the barcodes over the scanner on the desk, not taking his eyes off of her. Something about the way he was staring let her know he could tell she was lying.

"Why do you ask?"

Manny shrugged. "Gets dark out there at night. Eyes can play tricks on you," he said, nodding towards the mountains outside. "Anything else?"

"Um, yes, thirty dollars out on the pump. I'm not sure which number," she said, putting the snacks into her purse. "Listen, do you have a restroom I could use?"

Manny nodded and reached under the counter, then pulled out a key attached to a giant piece of wood. He pointed to the back left corner of the store, and Kate followed his direction.

She stood in the bathroom for a moment, staring at her reflection. The mirror was cracking around the edges and the bathroom smelled like cheap, industrial soap, but it was clean enough for a roadside bathroom. She turned the cold water on in the sink and splashed some into her face, being careful not to smear any more of her eye makeup. Her color wasn't good. *That's probably why he was staring.* Her skin was a pale shade that was bordering on green. Kate took a few deep breaths and gathered her resolve.

What you saw—what you think *you saw—was a trick of the light in the fog.*

She nodded at her own reflection as if to emphasize her point and convince herself, but her hands were still shaking a bit. She grabbed a paper towel, ripping it from the dispenser, and patted her face dry before walking out of the restroom.

When she did, she saw another man had joined Manny at the cashier's desk. He had the same dark features and large brown eyes, but his hair was shorter. The two men were whispering loudly, but became more quiet as she walked towards them. Manny shushed the other man, and they watched her walk down the aisle towards the front door. Kate's stomach turned as she walked towards the men.

She smiled tightly, doing her best not to show any fear. Setting the bathroom key back on the counter, she nodded at Manny and the man who had joined him. Manny smiled back.

As Kate pushed the doors open, she heard the men whispering again, as if they were arguing about something.

"Alright!"

The voice came from behind her and she jumped to look at the men. The other man spoke as Manny eyed him admonishingly.

"Señora, please," he said, shaking Manny's arm off of his back. "We need to talk to you."

Kate's stomach turned as she looked at the men with wide eyes. Her car was at the gas pump, at least fifty yards away. There was no way she could outrun them.

Manny, perhaps reading the fear in her eyes, spoke. He held out a hand to her. "This is my cousin Saul, Ma'am. He wants to talk to you. I told him to leave you be, but he insisted that this is important. In our family," he paused, looking at Saul, "My cousin is… I guess you might call it a Seer." Manny stopped and ran a hand through his hair, looking at the man next to him. "He senses things that most people can't, and when you were in the bathroom, he came out from the office and told me he saw something just now. Something about you."

Saul looked from his cousin, then back to Kate, and nodded solemnly.

Kate's eyes went from wide to incredulous. After the thing in the road and the eerie feeling at this gas station, the thought of some guy thinking he was psychic was the cherry on top of the most bizarre night she'd ever had. She paused for a moment, then took her hands off the doors and took a few steps toward the men. "What is it?" she asked, one hand clutching her car keys for dear life.

Before he spoke, he glanced from side to side, as if to make sure no one could hear. Confident that they were alone, Saul answered. "You saw one of them," he said.

Kate's mouth parted slightly, and she took a few more steps toward the men she was now sure meant her no harm. "Saw what?"

Saul motioned for her to come closer, and she did. Almost leaning over the desk to listen to him, he answered her in a whisper. "A Wendigo. A skin-walker."

Although Kate had never heard the term, her body was immediately covered in gooseflesh. She didn't look down to check, but she was sure that if she had, the little hairs on her arms would have been standing up straight. "What do you mean?" she whispered back in a choked voice.

Manny looked at his feet as the two talked and played with his fingernails. Kate could tell that he was nervous. She furrowed her brow at him, then turned to his cousin.

"What is a Wendigo—"

"Shh!" Saul cut her off. "Do not speak this word. I should not have even mentioned it myself. These things—the skin walkers— they wander these roads at night." He turned his head around again as if to confirm no one else was listening, then said, "They're hungry."

"Hungry?" Her face wore a look of confused horror.

"Do you know where you are?" Manny cut in. "In this part of the mountains?"

"Kind of," she responded cautiously, "I'm about twenty miles off the highway, somewhere in the Sierras."

"You've heard of the Donner party, right?" Saul asked.

Kate looked confused. "I do, but this is nowhere near where they got lost."

Saul shook his head. "Not them. Another group like them. The Lightwoods. Only a few people in the Donner party resorted to cannibalism, and that was after a long time with no food. The Lightwoods, though… it only took them a week to eat the first of their party. By the time a search party found them, there was just one left. He was completely mad, surrounded by the bones of his victims. The man was so insane that they shot him on sight and buried him right here in the woods, just up the mountain."

The three of them were silent for a moment as the men stared at Kate, waiting for her to respond. The fluorescent lights buzzed over their heads, the only sound in the otherwise quiet gas station.

Kate spoke up after a few moments. "What does that have to do with me?"

"Cannibalism is a sin against nature," Manny piped in.

"Not only was the man driven mad, but his soul is not at rest," Saul explained. "Consuming the flesh of another human forever marks your soul, and slowly, you become more like an animal than a man. When you die, you become one of them. Cursed to wander the earth. Forever. What you saw out there? What I *know* you saw? It was one of them. A skin walker."

Kate scoffed a little, doing a poor job of concealing her fear.

"I know how it sounds. Just trust me, and whatever you do, if you see it again, do not look it in the eye. That's how they entrance their victims, and then, when you're defenseless, they consume you. But no matter how many victims they devour, it's never enough," he said, looking back out the window towards the mountains.

Kate's bad dinner date now seemed like it had happened in another lifetime. Still, her tolerance for bullshit at this point was at an all-time low. In the most polite voice she could muster, she responded. "Skin walker, got it. Thank you for your concern." She gave them a smile and turned to walk out of the gas station.

"Ma'am, Señora, wait!" Manny cried, stepping out for the first time from behind the desk. He pulled something from his pocket and handed it to her. "Take this," he said. "It's a talisman for good. If you see the skin walker again, it might help you."

She looked at the object in her hands. It looked like nothing more than a smooth stone, the kind that cover creek beds, only it had a symbol carved into it. She did not recognize the symbol, but for a second the stone seemed to pulse warmly in her hand. Kate closed her fingers around it and gave Manny a kind of half smile, then nodded at Saul before walking back out the door.

The breeze hit her, and suddenly she was cold and alone. It was refreshing, though, to be out of the gas station and away from the strange cousins and their ghost stories. She shuffled quickly to her car and was inside with the door locked in record time. Kate took a few deep breaths and looked at her reflection in the rearview mirror. She didn't look much better than she had in the gas station bathroom. Kate realized she was still gripping the small stone Manny had handed to her, and placed it in a cupholder to her right. Exhaling through pursed lips, she started the car and backed out of the parking spot.

The road wound on down the mountainside, and fog was rolling in thicker than ever. She squinted and slowed down. There were only about twenty miles between her and the interstate which would lead her back home. *I can make it*, she thought. The radio was playing soft rock, and she reached to turn it off.

Her windows were open, and when she turned off the music, rather than the sound of insects buzzing through the pine trees, silence filled the air. Kate took a quick breath in and reached for the stone in the cupholder, squeezing the talisman in her right hand as she steered with her left. Static electricity filled the air, and once more she could feel the tiny hairs all over her body standing at attention.

No, not again, I don't want to see it again! she thought, suddenly frantic.

Kate looked at her odometer and tried to calculate how quickly she could speed to the interstate when a screeching sound came from somewhere to her left. She jumped, the steering wheel jerking in her hand, turning her car so that the left side tires were now hanging over the edge of the mountain road. Over the drop was a steep embankment, and she turned to look out the driver's side mirror.

The hideous face was there, the unholy combination between a goat and a coyote skull with flesh stretched tightly across it, riddled with holes and rot. It was staring at her with its mouth open, screeching. Kate screamed and jerked the wheel to the right to get all four tires back onto the road. The car fishtailed, coming to a stop in the ditch on the other side of the road next to a steep incline.

For a few moments, Kate sat there, trying to catch her breath. Trembling and still clutching the smooth stone in her right hand, she reached to put the car back into drive when she felt it again—

the prickling feeling of static electricity. Against her better judgment, she turned once more to look out the window.

It was there, though no longer screaming. It's horrible mouth full of jagged, sharp teeth was open towards her, as if ready to devour her at any moment. Kate's eyes widened, and she opened her mouth to scream as it reached one bony arm inside the car to grab her. She wanted to move, but something about its horrible black eyes prevented her. Kate felt as if she could stare into them forever, into their unending blackness. Then Saul's voice echoed in her ears.

"Do not look it in the eye."

The memory of the fear on Saul's face and the sincerity of his story jerked her back to reality. She broke eye contact with the creature and remembered the stone in her hand. Instinctively, she swung her right hand at the beast, holding the talisman out towards it. When the stone contacted its rotting flesh, there was a sizzling noise, and the creature screeched again as it recoiled.

As quickly as the thing had appeared, it vanished. The horrible screech faded to a dim echo in the woods, and Kate quickly closed her car windows. The thing was gone. She laughed maniacally, catching her breath, before bursting into sobs of relief. As she gathered her wits, a beeping sound came from the seat next to her, and she jumped.

A light shone dimly from in her purse on the passenger's seat. It was a new text message. She reached over and picked up the phone to read it.

"Listen, I'm thinking of giving you a second chance."

For a moment, she was confused, because the number wasn't familiar. Then she remembered. Her date. His words replayed in her ears —

"Check please!"

— only this time they didn't sting a bit. She could, she supposed, give him a second chance. After all, it's what a nice girl

—

a desperate girl

— would do. She picked up her phone, hands still shaking from the encounter with the Wendigo.

"*Screw off*," she typed.

Kate pressed send, tossed her phone into the backseat of the car, and peeled out onto the gravelly road. The sun was coming up, and she rolled her windows down, welcoming the cool breeze rolling through the mountains.

She laughed the entire way home.

RUN AWAY

The way John Brighton figured, he shouldn't have been in prison in the first place. So, when the opportunity presented itself, he up and left. His method wouldn't have flown in any of the larger correctional facilities, of course, but at a low-security prison in a one-stoplight town, it worked just fine.

It was their weekly time in the yard, and all twenty of the inmates who could leave their cells were playing a game of basketball while two prison guards pretended to supervise while chatting about their former high school football rivalry.

John was standing off to the side with a few of the less motivated men, while the rest of the inmates, twelve men convicted of various petty crimes, shuffled around doing their best to imitate men who could actually play basketball. Fat Mike dribbled right, Joe set a pick to block Larry, and, as Mike jumped for his shot, he bumped into Larry, who fell to the ground, swearing. Larry immediately jumped up, and as the ball swished through the rotting ropes of the hoop, he charged towards Mike.

"The hell's your problem?!" he said, shoving him with both hands.

Mike barely moved an inch. Larry had shoved him with all of his strength, but the name Fat Mike wasn't hyperbole. In a deep baritone, he replied, "No problem here, Larry." At the last word, Mike shoved him back with both hands.

Larry flew under the force of the shove and fell backwards onto Joe, who cried out in pain. Joe was pushing seventy, and his son, Junior, happened to be doing time with him.

Junior, who had been watching the game, jumped forward to help his father. As John watched, all the inmates charged towards the two now fighting on the ground and formed a circle around them. Punches were being thrown, and the sounds of groaning and fists contacting flesh and inmates falling to the concrete filled the air. Both of the guards finally caught wind of the fight and broke their conversation, rushing in to stop it.

"Hey! Hey!" the one guard yelled out, rushing towards the mob. The other soon followed behind, waving his nightstick and threatening to call the warden.

John just stared at them, sneering. *Animals*, he thought. *Every one of them.*

Something like a light bulb went off in his mind as the fight raged on in front of his eyes.

Every one of them. Guards included.

He turned around to look at the security fence, which backed up to a state forest bordering the prison yard.

Without a word, he took a few steps back. He glanced at the guards, who were now being held down by inmates who were taking turns throwing their own punches. John took a few more steps back and repeated the process until his back was against the fence. He watched the fight continue to escalate. Someone was bleeding, because he could see the drops forming a small stream that flowed towards him down the hill in the yard.

John's heart pounded in his chest as he turned around and threw himself at the fence, scrambling to reach the top before anyone saw him. He knew it wasn't electric. He'd seen enough squirrels crawling over the rungs from the cafeteria windows to know that. But he also knew there was a mangled mess of barbed wire at the top.

John didn't care. He climbed, making huge strides up the fence until he reached the top where the barbed wire hung. Still hanging there, he surveyed the rows of razors along the top, and decided that if he could avoid the major arteries—his groin, his wrists, and his neck—it would be alright. He'd bleed a little, but not enough to require medical attention.

Putting both hands firmly on the barbed wire, he bit down on his lower lip to avoid screaming. Sacrificing his palms, he swung himself up and over the wire in one motion. Once his feet were firmly on the other side, John bit down on his lip to muffle a scream and yanked his hands off of the barbed wire, feeling the metal prongs slide out of his flesh. For a moment, he hung there, watching the fight still going on in the yard, wincing as his hands bled.

The trees touched the fence, and the forest was thick, so even though he was hanging just on the other side, the tree branches afforded him some protection. Adrenaline coursed through John's veins. His mouth tasted like copper—a result of biting his tongue to keep from screaming.

Both hands still gripping the fence, he looked out at the prison. There were no sirens going off, so they didn't know he was gone. Yet. He knew that wouldn't last long, so he quickly climbed down and landed on the other side of the fence.

John held his palms toward his face. Neat rows of puncture wounds lined both hands, and his forearms had taken a few deep scratches, but otherwise he was fine. A serene feeling washed over him.

I'm free.

He clasped one injured hand over his mouth to muffle a joyful laugh, and winced at the pain. John took one last look at the prison and ran off into the woods.

He took several deep breaths as he ran, enjoying the natural smell of the woods, finally free of the musty prison smell. It was late summer, yet already that slightly sweet, dead-leaf scent of autumn permeated the air. Once he had walked about a mile from the fence, he slowed down a bit, stopping to rest on a fallen tree. He was in a clearing, and all was quiet except for the babbling of a stream somewhere in the distance. John remembered what he learned in the boy scouts.

Follow a stream, it will turn into a river. Rivers will lead you to people.

It wasn't so much *people* he needed to see, but he'd need food soon, and where there were people, there would be food. In the meantime, the stream meant he would at least have water. He put his hands on his knees and groaned as he sat up, unaccustomed to so much walking after nine months in a tiny cell.

John walked again, following what looked like had once been a trail carved out in the park, now narrow and overgrown. Branches brushed against him as he walked, and sticklers clung to his jumpsuit. Still following the sound of water babbling in the distance, he kept walking. Finally, he came to the bottom of a hill and found the stream. John smiled and sat down to catch his breath.

Small, silver-colored fish swam in its water. It was shallow, but wide. He looked down at his orange jumpsuit and prison sandals. Before he could convince any people, he might find to give him some food. He'd need clothes. He fumbled through his jumpsuit and brought out the lighter he had traded for back at the jail. Gathering what dry kindling he could, he lit a small fire and settled in for the night.

* * *

It had been a long three days. John wore a pair of too big Levis and a long-sleeved shirt he had pilfered off of a clothesline from a farm he passed, following the stream to the river a few miles back. He had thought about going to the house for help, but then he figured if they noticed he was wearing the clothes from their own line, well, that would be hard to explain. He had buried the orange jumpsuit unceremoniously in a shallow grave by the stream. Now all that was left to bury were his prison sandals, but he needed shoes, so he kept those.

He had finally arrived at the spot where the creek met the river, and it wound lazily down a hilly countryside. John stood at the top of the hill and smiled.

An old mill and a farmhouse stood surrounded by a few acres of tall corn. A man was working on a tractor and a woman stood sweeping off the front porch. An old tire swing swayed in the breeze from a tall ash tree in front of the house.

Farmers, he thought, smiling. He remembered his uncle, who had been a farmer and who had denounced banks. Instead, his uncle had stashed most of his cash on their property. If these people were anything like his old uncle, then it was simply a matter of sniffing it out. Probably under a mattress or in an old tin can somewhere in the house, but it would be there.

Just as the sun set, John smiled as he bent down to the river and splashed some water on his face. He used some more water to part his hair to the side, combing it in place with his hands. Tucking his shirt into his pants, he walked towards the farmhouse.

* * *

A tall but unassuming man answered the door in dirty overalls with a mouth full of dinner. "C'n I help you?

John smiled his most honest smile and shrugged. "Looking for work, I have experience on farms. Do you need any?"

The farmer looked to be in his seventies and wore a pair of dirt-caked jeans that were well worn at the knees and a short-sleeved work shirt. His blue eyes stood out brightly from under his cap, with deep lines set around them. The farmer studied John for a minute, looking him up and down, assessing him. He stopped when he saw the prison sandals still on John's feet, and John's stomach tightened. The man turned his gaze to John's and smiled warmly.

"We sure could use some help around here," he said, putting a hand out to shake. "Know anything about cattle work?"

"Yep!" John smiled, lying handsomely. "And I can start any time."

The farmer studied John's face for another minute before responding. "Well, that's just perfect. My name's Horace, you?"

"John," he said, putting a hand out to shake.

Some shuffling came from behind Horace in the house, and a woman's voice called out.

"Honey, what is it?"

"Got some extra help, dear! A John. Mr. John...?"

He paused for a minute, scrambling to think of a fake surname. "Green. John Green," he finally answered.

Horace smiled tightly. "It's a Mr. Green, honey!" he called out, opening the door and beckoning for John to come in.

He stepped into the house, and the smell of a warm meal hit his nose. His stomach groaned audibly, having eaten only some raw fish from the stream in the past few days.

Horace laughed and slapped John on the back. "Hungry, son? Lottie, fix up a plate for Mr. Green. We can put him to work faster if he's fed," he said, winking at John.

A skinny woman of around seventy shuffled from the dining room to the kitchen, still chewing her dinner. Horace led John to an empty seat at the table, and the men sat down. Lottie brought out a plate full of what looked to be some kind of meat pie and a tall glass of milk. John grasped them from her and drank the whole glass in great gulps. The meat was a little gamey, but he finished his plate in less than a minute.

She laughed, "Well! Someone was hungry." She sat down at her own dinner with a smile.

"We got another worker here, too. Tim," Horace said. "He's out in the shed, where you can stay, if you're of a mind to. There's two small cots in there."

John was barely listening, inhaling his second helping. "Hm?" he said, looking up. "That sounds great."

"Now, in the morning," Horace continued, "We'll need you up at four. That's when we ride out to the cattle for the morning feeding."

John looked back and forth between the woman and man and nodded, still chewing. He knew they were studying him, but he didn't care.

"One more thing," Lottie said, "You're welcome to come inside and use our facilities. There's a bath in the upstairs you can use once you're done with your work for the day. We just ask that you don't go up into the attic."

Horace had looked to look at Lottie as she spoke. When she finished, he nodded and said, "As long as you understand that, I think we'll all get along just fine."

"Sure," John said, swallowing, but the air in the room had chilled. The three of them sat in silence for a few awkward moments before Lottie perked up again.

"Well," she said, standing to clear the table, "I wasn't expecting a guest for dinner, but I'm sure glad you stopped by. It will be so nice to have an extra pair of hands around here." She smiled at the men as she collected their plates and walked them into the kitchen.

Horace picked up a knife and cleaned his teeth with it as John watched. "Yep, sure will be nice." He seemed deep in thought.

John cleared his throat. "I appreciate your hospitality. I worked on my uncle's farm every summer as a kid, so I know my way around things." He could hear dishes clanging from the kitchen as Lottie cleaned. "Say, do you think I could use that bath she mentioned?"

Horace broke his concentration and looked at John with a hint of alarm, and for a second, John was afraid the old man had forgotten who he was. "Of course, of course," he said finally, getting up from the table. "Follow me."

John pushed his chair back and did as he was told. The stairs groaned underneath their feet, and John grabbed ahold of the side railing as he walked, following the old man. The floorboards were wide and had clearly been set by hand.

Horace turned and said, "They sound creaky, but this is a sturdy house. Built it myself." He turned back around and kept walking.

John raised his eyebrows and continued following the old farmer until they reached the landing at the top of the stairs. This second floor was small and more like a loft than a second story. There was a bathroom in the corner and an even smaller room next to it that housed a sewing table and not much else. John looked up and saw a string hanging down from a hatch in the ceiling.

Horace caught him looking and said, "That's the attic. Remember, like I told you, stay out of there and we'll have no trouble. Bathroom's here. Towels are in the cabinet under the sink. When you're done, come down and I'll show you your sleeping quarters."

"Thank you," John responded, nodding and still staring up at the hatch. After a moment, he noticed Horace still hadn't moved to go down the stairs, so he turned his gaze from the ceiling. The old man gestured towards the bathroom, and John smiled again before walking in. He shut and locked the door behind him and turned on the bath, and the boards creaked once more as Horace lumbered back downstairs.

He turned on the hot water, and steam quickly filled the room. John wiped off the mirror and looked at his reflection. He couldn't believe they had let him in looking the way he did, with his face caked in dust and dirt. He had run the creek water over his face, but his cheeks and beard were still muddy, and it was clear he had been sleeping outside. John brushed his hands through his hair and undressed, stepping into the tub.

He winced at the heat as he slipped down into the water. For fourteen months, he had known only cold showers in the company of other prisoners, so it was hard at first to relax long enough to close his eyes in the bath. John tried to remember the last time he had actually bathed in a tub, and he figured it was probably back when he was a kid.

He soaked for a good forty minutes before draining the tub and drying off. Suddenly, a noise came from above him, from the attic. It was a clanking noise, as if chains were rattling together. There was another layer of noise too, and it sounded like faint, painful moaning. He scrunched his face as he strained his ears to make out the sound. Just then, a knock came at the bathroom door, and John jumped, water splashing from the tub as he did.

"Left you some fresh clothes, Mr. Green. Just some old long johns and work boots, but they're clean and dry," Horace called out from behind the door.

"Thank you!" John replied, eyeing his dirty pile of clothes on the floor. *Thank God*, he thought. John got out of the tub and dried off, and with the towel around his waist, he opened the door and reached for the clothes. He held them up to examine them. They were large for his build, but Horace was right—they were clean and better than a pair of jeans stolen from a clothesline.

When he got downstairs, the old farmer was waiting for him by the front door with a blanket. John smiled and followed behind as the old man led him outsides and towards a shed behind a large tree. It was dark now, and the moon cast inky shadows over the fields as they walked. John looked from side to side as he followed Horace across the grass.

They finally reached the shed, and for the first time, John saw the inside of what was to be his new home for the foreseeable future. The floorboards were made of mismatched wooden planks. There were no windows, and there were two single mattresses on iron frames with a small dresser between them. Still, it was better than a prison cell.

A middle-aged man with a gray beard sat on one bed reading from a worn Bible. He looked up at the men and nodded before going back to his reading.

"This is Tim, our other farm hand. He'll show you the ropes," Horace said.

"Pleased to meet you, Tim," John said, waving. He looked around the shed once more, studying it, and forced a grateful smile towards Horace. "This will work just fine, thanks," he said.

The old man smiled back and handed him a blanket. "Remember, first thing in the morning. Tim will show you around and you just help him. Come in at noon and four o'clock for lunch and supper."

John nodded. "Thanks again, Horace. I really appreciate it, and I won't let you down."

Horace studied him for a minute, as if the statement had startled him. Then he smiled tightly and nodded, saying, "See you in the morning."

When the door closed behind him, John made his way towards the bed. He had learned in prison that it was worse than foolish to talk to a man who was not interested in conversation, so he ignored Tim and got into the bed on the other side of the shed.

Tim flipped a page in the Bible and, without looking up, said, "I'll be getting you up at four. Got fifty hungry head of cattle to deal with. Then we'll tend to the field work. It's a small operation, but there's plenty to be done. You got experience in farm work?"

"Yeah," John said, "Helped on an uncle's farm every summer until I was eighteen."

Tim smirked, not looking up. "Then what happened?" he asked.

John turned to look at him, then laid back down in the bed. "Nothin. See you bright and early." He rolled over to face the wall. Tim kept the light on to read, but it had been a while since John had slept in an actual bed, so he drifted off quickly.

* * *

A month had come and gone, and John had settled into a routine. In the mornings, he woke before dawn and tended the cattle with Tim. Then they did a bit of fieldwork, and Lottie made them a pleasant lunch—usually a sandwich with some kind of meat on it, along with some fruit and cheese. They spent the afternoon back with the cattle, then they were back in for dinner. By the end of the meal, they were so tired that they stumbled back to the shed to sleep. Every other day, John would go upstairs after dinner to wash up in the bath. He noticed Tim never went upstairs, but figured that the guy was either a slob or woke up early to bathe before they fed the cattle.

On the last morning, the two of them sat in the bed of a truck out in the middle of the field. They were almost done for the day, and dinner would be ready soon. They were eating apples that had fallen off of a tree in the yard and sat in the comfortable silence to which the pair had become accustomed.

Tim smiled and looked off into the distance. "You make it up to the attic yet?"

Startled, John looked at him. "No. Have you?"

Tim ignored him and kept speaking. "A few nights ago, I thought I heard noise coming from up there, the sound of chains moving around, or metal crashing together…" he drifted off. "So that's a 'no' then?"

"No, man," John said, "They asked me not to."

Tim nodded and stared straight ahead. After a few moments of silence, he spoke up again. "I'll be leaving here in the morning."

"Yeah?" John asked, perking up, already planning to search the grounds and maybe even the house for some cash. It had been impossible to snoop with Tim around, and now that he was leaving, he would finally get his opportunity.

Tim nodded. "I am. In fact, I'll be gone before dawn. Listen, I tell you this because that means you'll be here alone after I'm gone. Just you and Horace and Lottie."

John took another bite of his apple and asked, "What's your point?"

Tim sat up and looked around, picked up a piece of straw from the bed of the truck and put it in his mouth, chewing on the ends as if choosing his next words carefully. After a few moments of silence, he spoke. "You ever wonder why people bother living so far out in the country, so far away from anyone else?"

John shrugged. "Privacy, I guess. I don't know, man. Who gives a shit?" he said, tossing the apple core out into the field.

Tim looked around before speaking again. "You should consider the fact that some folks have a reason for wanting to be so far away from others. Sometimes good reason."

John stopped chewing and looked over at Tim, who was still staring straight ahead.

"Is that a threat?" John asked.

Tim shook his head. "Nah," he said, almost laughing at the suggestion, before growing serious and looking back at the house behind them. "But this morning, my curiosity got the best of me, and I made my way up to the attic."

John's stomach tightened, though he couldn't quite explain why.

Tim turned to face him and said, "Son, I've been a field hand all my life, and I've worked at plenty of these little farms in the summers. Ain't a one of them ever kept a row of meat hooks in the attic."

John gulped.

"And I got to thinking, before you were here, there was another guy. We worked together just fine, and then, out of nowhere, one morning I woke up and he was gone. Horace said he took off in the night, and I never gave it much thought, but now..." he drifted off, spitting out the piece of straw. "I seen the marks on your hand. The neat little rows of scars? As a boy, I jumped a barbed wire fence and got some scars that looked just like those. But you're no boy, so the way I figure it, those scars mean one of two things: either there are plenty of people out looking for you, or ain't nobody looking at all. You need to think about which one of those outcomes is scarier, because I'm leaving tomorrow, and then it will be just you with these folks. And maybe that's not the best thing, if you're the kind of person no one would notice went missing. Understand?" Not waiting for an answer, he nodded and stood up. "Evening," he said, nodding before walking back to the shed.

John wiped sweat from his hands onto the front of his jeans. He thought for a moment, looking back at the house, and then across the field, towards the woods and the river which had led him to the farm. The house meant food and shelter and steady work, and probably cash if he could sniff it out. Then, a sound echoed in his ears from the night he had first arrived: painful moans, the clinking of metal chains coming from above him. From somewhere in the attic.

John jumped up from the bed of the truck and took off running towards the woods. He never looked back.

RITUAL

October 31, 1977

The four friends sat huddled in a small circle in the dark of Archie's parents' den. Their host was holding an old book in his lap, reading aloud. Three pairs of eyes were watching him, listening intently.

As the story ended, Archie turned the flashlight from the pages of the book to his chin, illuminating his face and making his features appear twisted and ghoulish. "And they were never heard from again," he said, letting out a high-pitched cackle.

"God," Penny groaned and threw her head back, her dark curls swaying. "You're a cheese ball."

Lorena sighed and crossed her arms over her chest. "This has been the most boring Halloween of my life."

Rick laughed, "Hey, I thought that last one was pretty good!"

She rolled her eyes. "This ranks right up there with the time you drove me four hours to see the world's largest Yo-Yo on our first date."

"That was fun, too," he grinned.

She shot him a look as Archie interjected, saying, "Lovebirds!" He picked the book back up and thumbed through it. "Come on, guys. Where's your Halloween spirit? Those were some classic tales! Lorena, tell me you didn't get a little scared, huh?"

She raised her eyebrows and shrugged. "Sorry, Arch. Those were lame."

The couples were seated on the brown shag carpet in Archie's den. The lights were off, but the curtains were open over the sliding glass door. Between the glow from the moon and the brightness from the streetlights, the room was awash in a dull blue haze, except for the one candle they had lit in the center of their little circle and the flashlight still in Archie's hand. His gaze was fixed on the book, his fingers turning its yellowed pages. Bound in dark leather, the book had creases along the binding, as if it had been well-loved.

"Where'd you get that thing, anyhow?" Lorena asked.

He looked up from the pages and gave her a mischievous smile. "Found it in a box in the attic. It was here when we moved in last year. Dunno why anyone would leave it, it's a pretty cool old book."

She grabbed it from his hands and closed it, blowing dust particles off of the cover. "'Ghost Tales of Worcester County,'" Lorena said, reading the title aloud. "Was that the last story?"

Archie looked down and furrowed his brow. "Actually, there is one more."

"Let me see that," Rick said, grabbing the book from Lorena's hands. He thumbed through it until he came to the last pages. "I knew it! Heaven's Victory Church."

Penny rolled her eyes. "Alright, Ricky, I'll bite. What's Heaven's Victory Church?"

His eyes lit up. "I can't believe you've never heard of it." Looking at the three faces around him, he could tell none of them had.

Archie eyed Ricky nervously as he spoke, but the girls looked interested for the first time that night.

"Out in the boonies, way past the interstate or anything like that, there's this deserted old church. One of those old revival ones, you know? Guys handling snakes and speaking in tongues—all that loony shit. It was founded by the first settlers in the area, but when people moved to the city, it was just abandoned. Now there's this old vacant church crumbling away with nothing around it for forty miles."

"So, what's the scary part?" Penny asked.

"Well, you can't get there using normal roads. You have to go off-road and you can't find it unless you go with someone who already knows where it is—it's *that* far from anything," he said.

"So, an abandoned old church in the middle of some cornfields, that's creepy enough, right?"

"I guess," Penny said, shrugging.

Rick's smile turned up in a devilish grin as he grabbed the flashlight from Archie's hand, turning it underneath his chin as his friend had. After a brief pause for dramatic effect, he continued. "I went there once."

"When?" Penny asked, her face crinkled in disbelief.

Rick looked at her. "When I first moved here, summer before freshman year. My brother got his license, and he'd heard about the place from some local kids. So, we went to check it out. It took us an hour to find the place, and when we did, it didn't look like anything special. Just an old brick church that was falling apart. We walked around, explored a little. Didn't find much. When it got dark, we headed home. We got in the car and, hand to God, as we drove off, I saw red lights glowing inside the church, like someone had lit some candles or something."

"So you just left?" Archie asked.

"We tried. The lights kind of freaked us out, so my brother got the truck started and we were on our way out of the clearing, when out of nowhere, this other truck comes barreling down at us."

The girls raised their hands to their mouths.

"No matter how fast we went, this truck was right on our tail. It chased us a good five miles and then backed off."

"Who do you think it was?" Penny asked.

He shook his head. "Never found out. They had their brights on the whole time, and we couldn't see anything through the glare."

Lorena scoffed. "You're messing with us. I've lived here my whole life and I've never heard of a '*Heaven's Victory*' anything."

"God's truth!" Ricky said, putting a hand on his chest. "Freaked my brother out so bad, he still won't talk about it."

Archie suddenly perked up, like someone had pulled a string attached to the top of his head. "Prove it," he said.

Rick was taken aback. "Prove what? How?"

"Take us to the church. To Heaven's Victory."

"Think you can handle it?" Ricky said, smirking at his friends.

"Let's go, Ricky," Lorena chimed in. "I'm so bored I could die."

Penny nodded in agreement. "We're in. Anything would be better than sitting here in the dark reading out of an old book."

"You're on," Rick said, smiling back at them.

They gathered their things and Ricky blew out the candle that was now burned down to a nub. As his friends stood up to leave, he watched as small wisps of smoke wafted up into the air. His smile faded. A vague sense of regret had crept over him.

* * *

The foursome bobbed along in Archie's dad's station wagon in the outskirts of Worcester County, Kansas, where the land is flat and boundless. They had turned off of the main roads twenty miles back and since then had been following wide, dirt trails which looked like horse and carriage rather than the wheels of any modern car had worn them down. The landscape was composed mainly of patches of brown grass and fields of weeds interspersed with the odd corn stalk.

Archie was at the wheel, shifting impatiently in his seat and eyeing the gas gauge. "I thought you said we were getting close, man."

Rick nodded. "We are," he said, pointing to a grove of trees in the distance. "Keep straight past those trees. It's tucked away back there." A shudder ran down his spine, which he tried in vain to ignore.

From the backseat came the pleasant cracking sound of a beer being opened. Penny took a swig and passed it over to Lorena, who sipped it daintily.

"Almost there?" Penny asked. The car went over a bump, and the girls fell back against their seat, giggling.

"Better be," Archie murmured. He slowed the car as they approached a grove of trees to the right of the path they were driving on, and the girls' chatter slowed as well.

"Here," Rick pointed, "Turn right at the trees. It's in there."

Archie looked at his friend in the passenger seat with concern before pressing the gas and driving the car through a narrow opening in the trees. As they passed through them, clouds gathered above their heads, casting a shadow over the already darkened grove. A building immediately came into view, and a barely audible gasp escaped each of their lips.

"No shit," Archie muttered, his eyes locked on the sight in front of them.

Rick nodded and said, "Told you."

Before them stood a white church in an advanced state of decay, its bricks eroded and the roof partially caved in. In front of it was a wooden sign with words hand-painted.

"HEAVEN'S VICTORY CHURCH, est. 1827"

Lorena kept her eyes on it while slowly reaching to open the car door.

"What are you doing?" Penny said, breaking her gaze from the church and turning to her friend.

"Don't you want to check it out?" Lorena asked her friends, who remained buckled in their seats. "Guys? Hello?"

The boys and Penny still had their eyes locked on the church. It loomed over them like a giant, even though the building itself was just one story tall. Despite its diminutive size, the church seemed to occupy all the space in the grove and emit a cool, unsettling vibration.

"Fine, you guys stay put, but I'm gonna look around," Lorena said, getting out of the car.

Her friends watched as she tiptoed towards the church. Penny and Archie shared a pensive look before they both made their way out of the station wagon. Ricky's gaze remained fixed on the building. Drops of sweat were showing on his forehead.

Archie shut the door behind them and he and Penny stood, arms at their sides, with their eyes pointed up at the old, crooked steeple which was tilted as if it could fall off at any moment.

Lorena was still ahead of them, now walking along the side of the church, running one hand along the white siding as she did, feeling the ruins beneath her fingers. She reached the end of the side of the building and craned her neck to look behind it. Without looking back at her friends, she took a step around the church into the yard behind it, and disappeared from sight.

Penny's lips parted slightly when her friend vanished to the back of the building. "We—we should see what she's doing." She looked at Archie, who had put his arm around her as they stood before the ruins.

He nodded. "Let's go."

The two of them crept slowly towards the church, hand in hand. After a few steps, Penny turned back to look at the car. "Rick?" she whispered, squinting, trying to see behind the tint of the car windows. "Ricky, you coming?"

Penny grabbed Archie's hand to lead him back to the car, but it slipped out and she didn't grab it again, instead continuing walking to the car. She moved quickly at first, then took more careful steps the closer she got to the vehicle. The sun had almost finished setting, and a fog had settled over the grove, covering the ground so that only the upper half of the car was still visible. She inhaled and took a final step towards the car, craning her neck to look inside. The waning sunlight and the car's tinted windows combined to make it impossible to see if Rick was still in there, so she reached for the door handle and flung it open.

"Rick!" she cried.

The car was empty. Her face twisted in confusion, and she stumbled back, falling onto her hands.

"Penny, get over here!" Archie called from the side of the church where they had last seen Lorena.

Still on the ground, she turned her head to follow his voice to the church, which suddenly looked like it was a mile away. She shut her eyes tight and then opened them, and the church and Archie were back to normal, just a few dozen feet from the car. Releasing a shaky breath, Penny wiped her hands on her jeans, got on her feet, and ran towards Archie.

"He's not in the car! Where did he go?" she cried.

Archie waved a hand in front of his face, trying to clear the fog that was creeping up around them by the minute. "He probably went out back to meet up with Lorena. I can't see for shit anyhow, can you?" Archie asked, leaning one arm against the side of the building to gain his bearings. Pieces of white paint chipped off the decaying brick and crackled to the ground when he did.

Penny shuffled towards him, looking towards the back of the church. The fog seemed to billow out from behind the building. *It looks like it's coming from a fog machine*, she thought. *If this is a prank, it's not a good one. Rick is never half as funny as he thinks.*

Penny walked towards Archie and the church. He was at the back corner of the building, peeking around to look at the yard behind it. Archie turned his head and called back to her, "I don't see Lorena!"

She quickened her pace to catch up with him before Archie was completely concealed under a cloud of mist. "It's too foggy. I'm sure she's back there. Lori?" she called out. No response came.

Penny made her lay to where Archie was and reached out to grab his hand. They shared a worried look before stepping together into the backyard.

The land behind the church was a small clearing which ended at the line of trees surrounding it. Fog encircled the area in big, sweeping gusts. All that remained of the sun was a flash of magenta peeking out from the treetops.

"Lorena?" Penny cried out. She let go of Archie's hand and took a step into the clearing. Her friend was nowhere to be found.

"Ow!" Archie cried from behind her.

She turned around, and Archie was sitting on the ground with his back against a large stone, clutching his shin. There was now a small tear in the lower right leg of his jeans, and a bright red streak of blood dripped from it.

"What happened?" she asked, stepping carefully towards where he was sitting. Her foot brushed a stone as she did, and she stumbled over it. Regaining her balance, Penny bent down to pick it up, but found that it was partially buried. She brushed a few errant leaves off and saw that it wasn't a stone at all. She gasped, raising a hand to her mouth.

The fog cleared around Archie briefly, and she saw he was actually leaning against a tall headstone. "I couldn't see it in the fog. Got a nasty scrape," he said, getting to his feet. He brushed the blood and dirt off of his hands and looked at Penny, who was studying the ground below them. For a moment, the two of them stood together, facing out into what they now realized was an old graveyard.

Only a few of the graves had tall monuments. The rest were rectangular and no bigger than bricks, laying flat on the earth. Penny bent down and brushed the dirt off of the stone directly to her right. The etchings were so eroded that she couldn't read them, except for the number 1836. She furrowed her brow and stood up, wiping her hands on her jeans.

"I don't think we should be here," she said.

Archie looked at her and nodded. "Let's find those two and head back. We can still catch the Halloween specials on TV if we're lucky."

The wind ripped around them, and more fog seemed to drift into the grove. A scratching sound came from the opposite side of the church, and they spun their heads to follow it. Penny walked in that direction, motioning for Archie to follow her. Together, they tip-toed across the old headstones to the other side of the church.

As they came around the corner, an old well came into view. The scratching noise was growing louder and seemed to come from deep within the earth. The two shared a confused, worried look. By now, the sun had completely set, and the only things filling the sky were clouds that swung lazily over the grove and a bright crescent moon. A beam of pale moonlight shone down, shining a spotlight directly on the well.

"What do you think that noise is?" Archie asked.

Penny took a step back, hitting the side of the church, unaware that she had been backing up from the well since they first spotted it. "I'm not sure," she answered. "Come on, let's walk around to the front."

"What if an animal has fallen down there or something?" Archie asked, his voice trailing off as he walked towards the well.

His voice suddenly sounded monotone and strange. Penny stayed where she was, her back up against the side of the church as she watched him. Suddenly, an owl cried out from the woods, and she jumped slightly, scratching her back against the building's rough brick facade. Her breathing intensified as she watched Archie approach the well and bend over the edge to look inside.

He jumped back, coughing and gagging as he bent over with hands on his knees. "God, what is that?" he cried. "It smells like something died down there."

"If it's dead, then what was that scratching noise?" Penny asked, alarmed. "Look, can we please head back to the car? I bet they're in there, laughing at us," she said, unable to conceal the fear rising in her throat.

Recovering from his gagging fit, Archie began searching the surrounding ground.

"What are you looking for?" she asked, exasperated.

He bent over to pick up a large, round rock. Pursing his lips, Archie turned back around and carefully dropped the rock down the well. He bent forward towards the well and looked to Penny.

"Listen!"

Both of them were silent for a few moments. Then Archie stood up completely straight and ran a hand down his face.

"Did you hear that?" he asked, searching her face eagerly.

"Hear what?"

"Nothing. I still haven't heard the rock hit the ground, or even the sides of the well. How deep is this thing?"

"I'm sure it fell in some mud or something. Let's go, come on," she said, her heart now pounding in her ears. Not checking to see if he was following, she kept herself flat against the wall as she walked towards the front of the building. Penny inched her way across the long side of the church until she felt the edge with her hand and, taking a deep breath, she turned the corner.

Churches typically inspired a sense of awe and beauty within her, but this one was grotesque somehow, unnatural. A set of stone steps led up to the front door, which was cracking and tilted to the side, no longer attached to the building itself. An old wrought-iron handrail hung lazily to the side, bent and warped horribly so that it almost touched the ground. Huge, dark double doors were pulled shut, a large wooden beam holding them in place. Penny felt hot breath on her neck, and she whipped around.

"Archie, what the hell—cut it out!"

No one was behind her. She peeked back around the side of the church towards the well.

No one was there.

"Archie!" she cried, tears welling in her eyes. No answer came, nothing but the fog that continued to roll out from the trees lining the grove. Her face twisted as she let out a choked sob.

"This isn't funny!"

A chill ran through her and she rubbed her hands against her arms to warm up. Goosebumps appeared on her flesh, and Penny took a last look at the side where the well stood. Then she turned to face the front doors again.

They must have all gotten inside somehow.

Penny stood at the steps and looked up. There was something painted above the entrance, and she squinted to make it out, taking carefully step at a time up the stone staircase. The fog had become so thick in the air that even looking down, she could not see her feet. At the stop of the stairs, she looked up at what someone had painted above the church doors.

The symbol, which had previously looked like an almond-shaped blob, was now clear to her. It was an eye, wide open and staring. Penny looked around, searching for a cross, a crucifix, any type of religious statue or monument, and found none. There was nothing but a single eye painted above the door, an eye that seem to stare back at her.

She turned her gaze from the eye and stared at the wooden beam holding the door closed. The fog was now impossibly thick, and Penny couldn't see much of anything except for the doors in front of her. The glow from the moon barely glowed through the mist, and her ears perked up as she heard a howl somewhere in the distance. Overhead, she could hear wings flapping, and she glanced up to see what it came from. A cloud of bats flew above her, moving in and out of the tufts of fog.

Penny took a deep breath and lifted the wooden beam before pushing the doors open. They protested, creaking and groaning as they swung to reveal the inside of the church. A cloud of dust flew out in her direction, and she waved her hands and coughed to clear her throat. Penny rubbed her eyes and squinted as the dust settled. She gasped loudly, the dusty air clinging to her lungs.

It's not real, it can't be real.

"My God," she whispered, raising both hands to pull at her hair. Her face was contorted in horror and confusion.

Before her were rows of wooden pews, rotting and dusty and ravaged by time. The floor boards were cracked, and cobwebs hung from every crevice. But that was not what terrified her, nor what shook her to her very soul.

The pews weren't empty. They were filled with the skeletal corpses of a congregation, all facing the altar. Some wore fancy burial clothes: suits, dresses, and fine jewelry. Others were covered only by gauzy, white burial shrouds.

Penny took a step back, unaware she was doing it, and stumbled. She caught herself before falling completely and looked back up at the pews. They were no longer full of skeletons, but horrific, rotting people, staring unendingly at the front of the church, where she followed their gaze.

Her friends, Archie, Rick, and Lorena, were facing away from her at the altar. A man dressed in a black suit and tie, rotting like all the rest, was standing next to them, holding a tattered old book.

The man's head snapped to the back of the church and locked eyes with Penny. Without a sound, he raised one arm and pointed at her. His jaw opened unnaturally wide as he unleashed a scream that immediately sent a wave of nausea rushing over her.

At the sound, her friends turned around to look at Penny.

She screamed wildly. Each of them looked like they had been in the grave for months. Their clothes were ragged, their skin tattered and grey, their eyes black and cavernous. At once, their mouths opened and they, too, let out howling screams. Penny turned to run, but not before several more of the creatures in the pews turned their heads to look at her, screaming in unison.

She practically dove out the door and down the church steps. Penny ran to her right, towards where they had parked the car. After a few minutes, she stopped and looked around. *If I can't see them, maybe they can't see me, either.*

The thought barely comforted her as she raised both hands to rest on her head while she caught her breath. Penny raised both hands and reached wildly into the fog. She couldn't feel anything in front of her, and she didn't know if she was even heading in the right direction. Completely disoriented, she wouldn't have known which way was up if her feet hadn't been planted on the ground. Taking another deep breath, she sprinted. Right as she took off, hands pulled at her clothes. Penny screamed and broke loose of them as she ran.

She coughed as she moved, her mouth filling with what she thought earlier was fog, but now felt more like smoke. It burned her lungs and throat, and she paused, bending down to put her hands on her knees and catch her breath. She waved both hands in front of her face, trying in vain to clear the mist from her vision. Now her eyes burned, and her breath quickened as she struggled to suppress a wave of panic.

Calm down. You can do this. You have two choices: stay put and suffocate, waiting for whatever the hell that was in the church to get you, or run until you can't run anymore.

Penny wiped tears from her cheeks and took off again. As she ran, she thought she could finally make out a shape in the distance.

Oh thank God, thank God, she thought as she got closer to the shape and saw that it was the car. It was still sitting in idle, and she could spot three shapes inside. *They've been waiting for me this whole time—those things in the church weren't real!* She continued her sprint towards the car and opened the door, throwing herself into the backseat.

She locked the door and shouted, "Go, Archie! Drive!"

But the car didn't move, and the mist was leaking into the car. She leaned forward to scream again. "We have to go, now!"

Penny froze. The car was slightly foggy, so she couldn't quite make out their faces, but her friends were each sitting, motionless, in their seats. Penny let out a small whimper and reached for the door handle.

As she did, a hand smashed against the window, followed by dozens of them. Bony, decaying hands were now clawing at the outside of the car. As Penny stared out the windows in horror, she suddenly felt eyes staring at her from within the vehicle.

Without moving her head, she turned to look at her friend.

Vacant sockets sat where Lorena's pretty brown eyes used to be, and her mouth was curled up in a sneer. Her skin was grey and bruised.

Penny screamed as Archie and Rick turned to her from the front seat. Their faces were like Lorena's—ashen and lifeless, twisted in scorn. At once, the boys climbed into the backseat, and the three of them clawed at her.

"Stay with us, Penny!" Archie cried, his voice aged and horrible.

"Stay forever!" Lorena screamed.

"You can't leave us, Penny!" Rick howled.

Penny was pushing herself back against the car door, scrambling for the handle, when suddenly the car door opened and she fell to the ground outside. Immediately, she was was pulled in all directions by clammy, clawing, bony hands.

As the undead dragged her back into the church, Penny screamed until her voice wore out. Her hoarse cries broke through the thick fog and rattled the trees surrounding the grove, shaking the birds out from the boughs and into the raven-black Halloween sky.

* * *

Officer Tony Richards was traveling down Rural Route 98 on the way home from his Halloween shift. He was exhausted and already considering how to get out of working next year's Halloween when he spotted a cloud of smoke to the right floating out over a grove of trees several miles off of the state highway. Sighing, he pulled over and put his car into overdrive to navigate the dirt field.

After nearly twenty bumpy miles, he pulled up to the grove and saw the source of the smoke. A station wagon was idling, tufts of grey smog floating out of the exhaust pipe. The officer looked around and lowered his head to speak into the radio.

"I'm going to need a tow."

Richards slowly approached the car and lowered his hand to the gun on his hip. Smoke drifted towards him and filled his lungs, and he coughed as he got closer to the car.

Exhaust fumes surrounded it so that he could not easily see inside. He paused. After twenty-five years on the job, it was rare that he was ever uneasy on a shift. In those years, he had learned to trust his instinct. When something felt off, it usually was. One hand still on his weapon, he turned off the safety and reached the other hand to the driver's side door. Holding his breath, he yanked it open.

The car was empty. He sighed heavily and rolled his eyes, lifting the radio to his mouth.

"Yeah, no one's in there. Just take it to impound."

He shook his head and began the walk back to the patrol car. He got inside and steadied himself, taking a sip of bad gas station coffee from a styrofoam cup.

"Goddamn kids. I hate Halloween," he muttered.

* * *

October 30, 1992

Ruth Hixton teetered on the edge of a stepladder in the attic. Just a few more inches and she'd be able to pull down the stack of board games the former owners of their house had left in a dusty pile on a top shelf. The air was scorching up here, and as she exhaled, specks of dust flew off the shelves. She coughed, and the dust made her sneeze just as she pulled the stack down with her.

They had expelled Ruth and her best friend from school. Since that meant she would miss the Halloween dance the following evening, she was planning a little party of her own. Her parents would be three sheets to the wind at the town's annual Halloween party, so they'd be none the wiser.

She jumped just a few feet to the floor, shook her head to clear the dust, and noticed a book laying open that had fallen down with the pile of games. Ruth closed it and examined the cover, tracing a finger along the embossed edges as she read the title out loud.

"Ghost Stories of Worcester County."

She flipped the book open and thumbed through it, stopping at the last story. There was a map and a picture of a small, white building behind a row of trees.

"Heaven's Victory Church."

She studied the map closely for a few minutes before realizing that it was within driving distance. An idea struck her. Tomorrow night, she and her friend would not regret missing the dance, and they wouldn't be stuck playing board games, either. Ruth bounded down the attic stairs and picked up the telephone. She dialed the number and got an answer right away.

"Cindy? It's me. Listen, forget the party." She held the book up and examined the map, breaking into a wide grin. "Tomorrow night, we're going exploring."

"*Walking After Midnight: Tales for Halloween Part I*" available NOW at most major retailers.

Part III Coming 2022!

Go to www.evancamby.com to join the free monthly newsletter.

Note From the Author

Thank you for taking the time to explore my little collection of short stories. I hope you had as much fun reading as I had writing them.

Oh, and I hope you had a few scares.

If you've enjoyed this book, would you consider giving it a review or sharing it with a friend?

I appreciate your readership.

Until next time,

Evan Camby

Made in United States
North Haven, CT
16 September 2022

24217669R00082